STAFF

Jeff Wedgle

STAFF
by Jeff Wedgle

Dook Dook Press
Denver, CO 80224
orders@dookdookpress.biz; http://www.dookdookpress.biz

ISBN 978-0-578-02331-1

First Edition 2009
Printed in the United States of America

Wedgle, Jeff.
STAFF
The most powerful biblical object falls into the hands of Evil in the 21st Century – 1st ed.

Dedicated to all believers in The One God... extremists excluded

To Snoop, Rikka, Cubs and Dook Dook

1
Jerusalem, 35 A.D.

The haggard old man peered through the door, fearful of confirming what he already knew. He looked up and down the alleyway, one of hundreds in this ancient city. Though he couldn't see them, he certainly heard them, for he was trained to listen for their distinct march. Indeed, the Romans were on their way and the old sage knew what they were after. Word had gotten out.

"*How?*" he half-muttered to himself as he swiftly but silently closed the door, careful not to disturb the silence. The frail old man knew he had to act quickly. The Romans would be here soon. And once they discovered which home was his, their rage would escalate until they found what they were looking for. Somehow on his own, he must get it out of his home immediately.

Even compared to the poor conditions of the time, his home was well below what was considered poverty. Material possessions, already scarce, were noticeably less existent in this home. He didn't need much anyway. He was a spiritual man, known by his people to be one of the *thirty-six*; the number of righteous people needed to keep the world from destroying itself. The holy sage lived his life more in the spiritual realm than the physical; dedicated to God, engrossed in the wisdom of his faith, while living and discussing the teachings with his disciples.

The great sage thought about the question again. *"How could word have leaked out of the room that night?"* The question nagged at him as he nervously moved about the small front room of his two room home. It was impossible to think anyone present that night could be held even remotely responsible.

For most residents of the community, that particular night was an ordinary Jerusalem summer night, but for the sage, his five sons, and immediate disciples, it was anything but ordinary; in fact, it was most intense, as decisions made in the room that night would determine the fate of the world. The group was already accustomed to witnessing incredible occurrences, as time would later prove them to be some of the most turbulent events in world history. These events would forever change the religious beliefs of the world's inhabitants. History was being written daily, and all who lived in Jerusalem were helping to write it. In the middle of it all was Honi, a dedicated disciple of the great sage. It was Honi, along with his bloody and starved body who had brought *it* into the sage's home.

Honi had been dispatched with the daunting task of finding the Holy Relic. If he didn't, then the Romans would surely discover it, as they were already excavating beneath the Temple Mount within two hundred yards of where it was believed to have been hidden. Three days had passed since Honi set off through the secret opening into the great catacombs that lay beneath the holy Temple Mount, the base beneath the holiest site of the Jews. His food and water supply were lost twenty hours before, when he had fallen asleep and the rats had come. The food, crusts of dried bread to prevent spoilage, was already devoured before he was jolted awake by the stinging sensation coming from the top of his left thigh. He awoke to the nightmare of seeing his body as the provision for two hungry rats, enticed by the smell of blood trailing from an open wound. Honi furiously swatted the rats aside, jumped up and began to run. He quickly regained his composure, realizing he needed to go back and retrieve the lamp and oil supply that remained at the resting spot- the only items not contaminated by rat saliva. The rats were still congregated there and Honi shooed them away to retrieve his belongings. Now that he was fully awake, he warily resumed his way through the great labyrinth.

Honi fought hard to hold back the oncoming surge of panic as he thought of nearly losing the lamp and oil flask- his only possessions for hope and survival. Doing so would guarantee no chance of return, inviting a slow death in pitch blackness. Then there were the rats. They would most certainly return once they smelled the decay of his body. More than once, Honi choked down the bile rising in his throat when he thought of being eaten to the bone by the rats. He shivered to think how he too might become part of the hidden treasures buried in the great catacombs- the endless network of tunnels that lie beneath the Temple Mount. He thought about dying alone, about waiting centuries before his remains would be found, only to wait that long for a proper Jewish burial, and that would only be if he was discovered by his own people. He had to succeed.

It wasn't that the catacombs were long that made them arduous. It was the incredibly complex maze of seemingly endless paths built by his ancestors that made the task so prohibitive. All too often he would take a wrong turn, ultimately forcing him to retrace his steps and start again. No map had ever been made of the artifact's location for fear of it being discovered by the enemy. In fact, for centuries, the only knowledge of the catacombs and the whereabouts of the Holy Relic was taught orally from generation to generation and even then, known only by few.

This massive cache of antiquities lying below the holiest place in the world for the Jews was of particular interest to the Romans, who learned of it through studying Jewish texts and tradition, and paying handsomely for the information. In the year 586 B.C. the First Temple, standing exactly where the Second Temple now stood, was besieged by the Babylonians under the reign of King Nebuchadnezzar. Sadly knowing what fate lay before them, the Jews of First Temple times built the catacombs in an attempt to hide their holy vessels that once filled the Holy of Holies- the sacred inner chamber of the Temple.

The Holy of Holies was prohibited from anyone entering, save the High Priest and even he was only allowed to enter this sacred place but once a year, on the holiest day of the year, the Day of Atonement. It was on that day, inside the Holy of Holies, that the Priest would pronounce the hidden name of God. Many priests, however, were not worthy of surviving such an honor, and died at the mere utterance of The Name. Some of the vessels had managed to be hidden. Most did not and were carried off to Babylonia and publicly displayed as a show of the victory over Jerusalem.

Exhausted, Honi sat down against the cold stone walls of the giant maze to rest. His fear was momentarily subdued by the awe of comprehending how his ancestors could create such a place.

Thoughts of his demise mixed with the awe of how this place was created switched back and forth in his mind. Honi passively peered at the stones in the wall opposite him. As he focused on them, the stones in the middle of this section of wall appeared different somehow. They lay ever so slightly off center, just enough to produce a tiny protrusion out from the rest of the wall. To anyone else it would have gone unnoticed, but Honi was trained to look for subtleties and he knew these stones had been moved.

Honi stood up, never blinking as he waved his small oil lamp back and forth in front of the wall as he further scrutinized the stones. He chose one and pushed hard against it. Small pebbles dropped from its sides. Without hesitation, Honi clutched the oil lamp between his teeth, freeing both his hands to claw around the sides of the rock. With no tools to assist him, he committed his bloodied fingers to remove the stone. Prying and pulling for what seemed like an eternity the stone eventually budged, and elation poured into his soul compelling him to continue with greater fervor. Honi persisted through the pain moving the stone, watching as millimeter by millimeter he managed to free it from its centuries-old resting place. At last the stone was positioned just enough for Honi to get a grip on all sides of it with the ends of his fingers. Compared to the rest of the stones surrounding it, the stone was small, but it was still dreadfully heavy. An hour passed before he finally managed to break the stone completely free from its confinement. During a final, labored pull, Honi lost his grip and the rock plummeted to the ground, clapping a startling echo through the tunnel. Fear poured into him like water from a bursting dam as he stopped breathing and listened intensely for sounds of the Romans, whom he pictured hearing the loud thud of the dropped stone and consequently setting off to investigate. To be discovered would bring instant arrest, no trial and death by crucifixion. But the fear of Pilate gaining control of this sacred article was greater than being discovered, and courage displaced his anxiety. Pontius

Pilate, the maniacal Roman governor of Jerusalem wanted the Staff, and his reputation held true that pitiless torture was the means to get what he wanted.

Minutes passed like hours as he removed the surrounding stones. Honi trembled as he struggled, digging away at the dirt and mortar that enveloped each stone. Mumbles of prayer for both thanks and mercy left his parched lips.

Honi stuck the lamp into the hole that he had just created. Bugs and spiders, scared by the centuries unseen light source, scurried to find new hiding places. One meter beyond his reach, the light revealed the shape of a long object, two yards long and encased by a shroud. In order for him to attain it, Honi needed to remove more stones. He poured the remaining oil into the lamp leaving the flask empty. Time was of the essence.

In what seemed to be an eternity, he finally created a gap just big enough to squeeze through. Honi climbed into the newly-made crevice. Laying sideways, his body wedged between the rocks up to his chest, Honi strained his arm as far as pain would allow. He almost dislocated his shoulder from its socket as his hand glanced the side of the shroud. Honi's trembling fingers made it far enough to nudge at the top of the relic, rocking it toward him. After a painstaking effort, Honi extricated the object. The first touch with the holy object sent surges of raw energy throughout his body. Honi knew what he was holding. He knew the power it possessed. He scratched and scraped his way out of the hole in the wall while at the same time holding the artifact as one would a newborn baby, taking great pains to get it out without the slightest contact of the relic against anything but his hand.

Once out, he cradled the sacred vessel in both hands. It took every ounce of his mental strength to overcome the immense desire to unwrap the shroud and gaze at the consecrated object. But Honi knew he could not, since just by carrying it he already felt its holiness and power. Ancient tradition didn't fail. It had brought Honi to the exact hiding place of the actual Staff- the instrument of the exalted prophet, Moses, who had once used it to perform the greatest miracles and plagues mankind has ever known.

2

    While the old sage thought of what to do, the night's onslaught had started. The Romans performed their search of the old houses in the manner which made them famous; they meticulously searched every crevice of every house and the inhabitants as well. Women were defiled in front of their husbands and children. Anyone who protested was immediately met with the sword. Hundreds died that night. Others were taken into custody for questioning. Still others were brought before Pilate himself.

    Though the old man knew he could put a stop to the merciless behavior by handing over the Staff to the Roman soldiers, he knew even greater evils would befall his people, as well as the rest of the world, if he were to do so. Moving as quickly as his brittle body possibly could, the sage went to retrieve the Staff.

    He entered into the smaller, second room of the two-room house. With the exception of a lit oil lamp, a rug underneath a small, wobbly oak table and two accompanying chairs, the room was vacant. The frail little man walked painfully up to the table and attempted to move it. Time simply did not permit the old man to find additional help. He knew the soldiers would be at his house within minutes, if not sooner. With every ounce of what little strength he had, the old man labored to move the small, heavy table inch by inch until he had moved it far enough to push the carpet to one side. Under the carpet was a section of floor that had been modified with a removable door, eighteen inches square. Carved into the door was a little space, just big enough to insert two or three fingertips, to lift the hatch out and away from its normal position. Though his energy was nearly exhausted from moving the table, the old man still needed to lift the cumbersome entry in the floor. Daunting as the task was, he managed to open it, mostly because the holy old man knew this was to be his final test in the physical world.

"God is giving me the strength," he meditated to himself as the door slowly moved away to reveal an opening in the floor. The man took the oil lamp as he descended down the rickety ladder to a secret room five feet below. Originally, the room was no more than four feet squared, but once it was determined to be the hiding place of the Staff, an additional few feet were quickly dug out to accommodate its extra length.

The remainder of the room was filled with broken down shelves that barely held its contents- old parchments of various sizes. Loosely arranged and in no particular organizational order, they held the secrets from Judaism's mystical side, the Kabbalah, and were of no value to anyone except the devoted students of the faith. Even still, the Roman Empire considered them to be a real threat. This particular set of parchments was one of only two known to exist. The risk was great for anyone in possession of them. If one was discovered to be in possession of such materials, the owner would be crucified and the material burned. The Romans trusted no one. Since Jerusalem was a powder keg of religious and political furor, those who practiced Judaism were feared to become rebellious and incite public demonstrations and other acts of defiance against the Roman occupation.

As the sage took hold of the shrouded Staff he felt the power and awesomeness that emanated from it, just as Honi did. He too had never unwrapped the shroud. There was no doubt in the old man's mind the Staff had a consciousness all its own. The immediate challenge for the old man was then to hold the Staff as delicately as he could while climbing up the ladder. Grasping the ladder with one hand while holding the Staff with the other, the old man arduously climbed the rungs back up to the room. Halfway up he managed to place the Staff on the floor still above his head, stabilizing himself with his newly-freed hand. As quickly as he could, the sage climbed the remaining rungs of the ladder, relieved as he emerged back into the room. No time was to be had to return the room back to its original state. This was the hardest part of all for the old sage, since he knew that keeping the

Staff out of the Roman's hands would be paid with the heavy price of seeing the sacred parchments destroyed. It was inevitable the soldiers would find this room, and consequently set fire to the house and its contents.

If there was any chance to prevent the Staff from falling into Pilate's hands, the sage knew he must entrust it to someone of the next generation, since the strength and endurance of youth was a requisite to bring the Staff to its new chosen place of rest. He needed to get the Staff to Levi, the sage's third eldest son.

Levi, who lived just two alleyways down from his father, was a scholar and the only son not yet married. He lived alone, dedicated to his faith, composing some of the few Jewish writings permitted by the Empire. Since he was alone, Levi assumed the responsibility of looking after his aged father. He knew his father had many disciples, all were more than willing to care for him, but Levi knew that caring for one's parents was part of the *commandment* of honoring one's parents. He knew that merits received by obeying the commandments were the only items one could take with them to the next world. Knowing this, Levi did this and all of God's commandments with great joy. Furthermore, since his brothers and only sister were already married with children, it seemed only natural to take on the responsibility. The old man knew Levi was the natural pick to perform the task of taking the Staff.

With the Staff guarded in his hand, the sage struggled to climb out the back window of the house, knowing an unfortunate stumble or fall would be fatal to him and the rest of the world. From the window, he fumbled through a winding row of stone archways, past the old dilapidated structures his community called their homes. Not too far off in the distance, he could hear the terrifying sounds of the Romans' onslaught. Screaming mothers, crying children and soldiers furiously barking- all culminating into a single, horrible requiem. It seemed, the old man thought, as if Pilate had sent the entire Roman Legion into this humble community to retrieve the Staff.

"One more house," the sage assured himself as he urged his failing body forward. He rounded the corner into another alleyway and limped quickly through a once beautiful stone archway to get to Levi's door. Once there, he knocked with a hushed frantic cadence. Levi opened the door.

His son was still dressed even though the hour was late. It wasn't unusual that Levi would work well into the night. Of the old sage's five sons Levi had always been the most devoted to the faith, which was the reason he had never married. His passion for the mystical side of Judaism drew him into a relationship with the Divine that no woman could coexist with. This relationship was one that was infinitely more fulfilling than any physical pleasure could offer in this world. His meditations drew his soul closer to the Creator, and it was known that Levi could go days without food or water during these meditative periods. His level of closeness far surpassed his fellow students of Kabbalah. They knew this endurance was a direct result of Levi's ability to have achieved a tremendously high level of closeness with God.

"Abba!" Levi cried as he saw his elderly father nearly collapse as the door opened. The old sage stood at the entryway, cradling the Staff with his left arm, his right arm holding him up as his hand clutched the outer walls of the entrance for support. Levi quickly grabbed his father's waist to support him before he fell. Using his other arm, Levi quickly wrapped it around his father's legs, and carried his father into his house. The Staff never left the old man's grasp.

"Abba!" Levi cried again as the tears welled up in his eyes and streamed down his cheeks. For many times and many reasons, Levi had seen his father in pain.

"They found out?" Levi asked knowing the answer already as he looked at his father holding the Staff with clenched fists. He guided the old man to the bed, urging him to rest. Levi had been in the room the night Honi brought the Staff back from the catacombs. In his heart he knew it would only be a matter of time before the inevitable occurred. Levi begged his father to let him watch over the Staff, but the old man steadfastly refused. The holy sage knew Pilate was a monster, and the old man had witnessed firsthand what horrible tortures the Roman governor's sick mind could conjure up.

"Levi," the old man laboriously gasped, "I'm sorry, my son."

Crying uncontrollably, Levi answered back. "Please Abba, don't be sorry."

"The fate of the Staff rests with you now, my son. You must get it to the new chosen hiding place."

"But to where Abba? We've not had a chance to find out where it should go. I am afraid I will fail," Levi returned.

"If you do, it is because it is God's will," whispered the great old man. "You are one of His most highly prized sons of man. If you fail, it is only because the Master of Heaven has another plan. Do not be afraid."

Levi looked down to the ground as if trying to summon the courage somewhere from the floor.

"But... I must stay here and take care of you," he pleaded.

"No, my son," the old man shook his head. Lying on the bed, the sage stared straight into the pupils of Levi's reddening, watery eyes. "I have completed my life's mission. No task can be of greater importance than getting this Staff to someone who can take it from here and I have accomplished that task. I have delivered it to you, my son. My time in this world has come to an end. I have loved you more and more every day, since the day you were born. I loved you even more when your mother died. And I love you most of all now that I am about to die."

Levi needed no explanation. Jewish tradition had taught that the great masters knew when their time was to expire, and could bring upon the passing into the Next World at will. The day Levi anticipated for years had finally arrived.

"I love you, my master, my teacher, my father."

Upon hearing the words spoken by Levi, the old man smiled through his dried, cracked lips at his son. As his speech faded, barely audible, the old man spoke to his son for the last time. "Be only of strong courage... The Master of the Universe is with you! Follow His path always. Tell your brothers and sister that I love them so much. I look forward to being with all of you in the Next World. I love you." The sage then said the Shmah, the affirmation of the One God. And with those words, the soul of the great sage left his body.

3

Levi stood over his dead father. The old sage's eyes were wide open, staring blankly to the Heavens. Levi extended two trembling, cold and dry fingers to lightly pull the eyelids closed. Levi was conflicted between bereavement and disbelief. The reality of the night was now palpable. The sounds of screams escalated, ripping through the night, leaving little to the imagination. The Roman assailment left no time for Levi to mourn. He kissed his holy father's forehead and put his arms around the lifeless body, wailing in muffled agony as he held the honorable sage for the last time. Prying the Staff from his father's grip, he cried profusely, stripping the sheets from his bed and rolling them over the body, completely concealing it. He knew precious seconds remained before the Romans would be at his door. The mission of the Staff had been thrust upon him before he even had time to consider what to do. Levi stole one final moment to glance back at his father's lifeless body, now wrapped in sheets, and hastily ran from his home. As stealthily as he could manage, Levi darted down an alleyway in the opposite direction from where he thought the Romans were coming. The more he ran, however, the more Levi became cognizant of the screams and horse hoofs coming from every direction. He knew this meant only one thing- the Romans had completely surrounded the entire Jewish neighborhood.

Levi ran towards another alleyway entrance, just fifty yards to his left. Once there, he sprinted as fast as his lungs could supply air, arriving at a crumbling staircase that linked to a worn circular cistern that once served as a main water supply for the city. Though old and in disrepair, it proudly stood four stories tall and could be seen from miles away. The top of the tank was one of the highest points of this part of the city, and boasted a clear vantage point of Jerusalem.

The steps wound around the cistern, separated less than two feet from its walls and desperately in need of repair. Originally, the steps were built solely for the purpose of providing regular maintenance to the tank. Though aged, it still contained and supplied thousands of gallons of drinking water to the poverty stricken neighborhood. The outer walls featured a myriad of patchwork, as the inveterate silo had seen its share of destruction and rebuilding. Armies seeking to take control of Jerusalem would often target such structures, smashing holes in them to release the water, while flooding the surrounding homes and eliminating the drinking supply, which paved the way for the slow death of thousands of men, women and children. As one army defeated the one before it, such was the regular cycle of events for Jerusalem, The City of Peace.

Levi remembered a small supply room housed at the top of the staircase. He recalled the room contained window openings where he would have a vantage point to look over the city's eastern side enabling him to determine a safe passage out of the city. Levi scurried up the dozens of stairs, as they laboriously wound along the giant circular walls of the cistern. At the top of the steps, the supply room was situated six feet straight ahead.

The supply room door was held shut by a small rusty iron latch that locked from the outside. Levi pried open the latch and slowly peered inside. The room was dark, but a small amount of firelight crept in from the window on the other side of the room. It was far larger than he expected and was littered with hundreds of medium-sized canvas bags of ground up Jerusalem stone, used for patching the cracks in the cistern walls. The bags had been carelessly stacked four and five high, rows of them filling most of the room. The rest of the interior hosted an assortment of various tools and barrels; some with water and some empty, used for mixing the paste to repair the tank. Levi briefly pondered why a new cistern was never built, but as fast as the thought entered his mind, it was suddenly replaced by the more pressing matter of planning his escape from the city. Quietly, he entered the room and closed the door behind him. The door remained slightly ajar as it could not be completely closed without latching it from the outside. On the opposite side of the room, shabby wooden shutters attempted to hold back the cool air of the night in vain. Levi maneuvered around the loose piles of bags, sidestepping around them to get to the window.

The shutters were held in place with rusty latches capped by black rings. Levi pulled hard on one which created undesired friction upon its release. Finally, he was able to free the latch and open the shutters just enough to investigate the city. Looking out over the eastern section of Jerusalem, the dim city looked amazingly empty considering it was the home to thousands. It was too dark for Levi to see much. A few hundred yards in the distance, through the sunless city, he viewed a large semicircle of flames from torches encircling the eastern half of the city. Though it was not possible to see the other side of the city, Levi knew that the other half of the city would likewise be encircled by flames. He knew the Romans had surrounded the city, allowing no one to leave. The probability of getting the Staff to its new chosen hiding place, outside of the city, was diminishing with each precious minute.

Despair poured over Levi like oil. Seeing the colossal sized ring of soldiers encircling the city made Levi think his attempt to escape the city and get the Staff to its chosen site would be futile. It would be so much easier, he thought, to find a way to hide the Staff within the city itself. That possibility had been considered the night Honi brought the Staff to his father's house. But it was quickly dismissed since most in the room knew of the jealousies that the invading armies had for Jerusalem. Once conquered, the new residents would quickly inhabit the nicer dwellings, while razing the unwanted structures and building new ones in their place. The Staff would either be discovered or destroyed if it were to remain hidden within the city. No- it must be hidden as far from man as possible if there was to be any hope of keeping it out of the hands of evil.

In the relentless deluge of ugly background noise, Levi heard the Roman soldiers at task, searching for the Staff. Nausea set in as he looked at the holy object, the object for which so many were being slaughtered that night. Tears which Levi didn't think he had again welled up in his eyes as he thought about the loss of life of his people.

He thought about his father again and wondered if his siblings would find their father before the Romans did. The Romans knew the sacredness of the Staff couldn't be entrusted to just anyone. They were well aware of who the religious leaders of the community were, and targeted them with the initial onslaught. Perhaps, he wondered, that his father's ability to get out of his own house and die at Levi's was the blessing that bought the time necessary for his siblings to recover his father's body before the Romans. With this in mind, Levi found the strength needed to focus and devise a way to get out of the city.

4

Nachum, son of Nachum, was a wealthy and conceited man. The characteristics he possessed were family traditions handed down from his father. Like most of the other Jews, the elder Nachum started out poor. But unlike his fellow Jews he was not the least bit interested in adhering to the Jewish laws refraining from conducting business on the Sabbath. He also contradicted the community's accord of refraining from business transactions with the Roman occupiers. It was actually the latter of these which brought Nachum the senior to affluence.

Nachum the elder was in the metal household wares business. Copper and iron plates, forks, knives and the like were found in great abundance from Nachum. On the Sabbath morning he would go off to the market to sell. But he left very early in the morning since, before market, he was oftentimes with the occupiers, answering any question posed to him. He then worked with the Romans to educate them on the ways of the Jews. That in turn provided them with a great advantage when strategizing the occupation. To make his meetings look natural, he brought along his wares for which the Romans gladly paid him handsomely. He would then go along to the market and sell more. Between the two, the day of rest became a very lucrative day.

He would then return to his community, boasting of the great business he was doing in spite of his nonobservance to the Sabbath. When the other tradesmen, immersed deeply in their faith, saw Nachum and his improved quality of life as a result of violating the Sabbath, they were undeniably allured to wonder how much better they might do if they also broke from the laws of Judaism. Ultimately they refused the temptation, but Nachum persisted. As a result, he prospered financially and was able to enjoy the finer side of life. The elder Nachum married a woman twenty years younger than he, and their union managed to produce one child, a son whom he also named Nachum in honor of himself. Such was not the practice of Jews to name their child of the same name. But since Jewish law mattered little to this man, he felt no guilt whatsoever by giving his name to his child.

He raised his son to be just as materialistic and arrogant as he. The younger Nachum eventually proved to be even worse because he had two additional qualities that his father lacked; youth and handsomeness. Women hated him, but somehow found themselves in his home in intimate relations due to his charm. More often than not, their hopes of long term romance or marriage were cut painfully short as they were often ordered out of his house only moments after Nachum attained sexual satisfaction.

Though the younger Nachum lived among the Jews rather than with the statesmen of Rome, it was out of a sense of power and control as opposed to one of community and brotherhood. Thus, when he was awakened by the din of that dreadful night, he immediately rushed outside to determine who was responsible for his inconvenience. The scene outside was one of chaos and rage. Though held in high esteem with the Roman occupiers, Nachum feared his status might be forgotten for even a slight moment and that he too would become a casualty of the night. He hurried back inside and dressed himself. He quickly left his home and turned into an alleyway leading him to the stable that housed his prized white stallion- a gift from Pilate himself for his 'dedication'. He saddled the horse and quickly rode off toward the perimeter of the city, away from the Roman army.

When he reached the city's edge, Nachum saw an unusually large group of soldiers guarding the city's exits. Upon further investigation, he witnessed the men questioning anyone trying to enter or leave, as they searched every container and garment which could be used as a means to smuggle the Staff out of the city. The disorder was much less intense here than where his house was, as the city's perimeter was not populated with any houses. These areas hosted the stables and pens that sheltered the animals. Nachum ordered the horse to approach the Roman sentry who was overseeing the interrogation. It was rare for any of the Jews to own a horse, let alone a horse of such quality. The guards diverted their attention away from their immediate task as they saw Nachum, crowned upon his possession, striding toward them.

"In the name of Pilate the Great, I bid you salutations," Nachum called out to the lead guard. He possessed amazing talent for making patronizing comments come across as sincere.

"Who are you that possesses such a great animal?" the guard responded as he looked up and down at the rider and his stallion.

"I am Nachum ben Nachum," he replied. Nachum always felt a surge of pride whenever he told someone who he was. The response was always the same.

"You are Nachum the merchant who has a personal audience with the Governor?"

"That is I," Nachum replied confidently. "Tell me what you seek that is of such importance that this inquest could not wait until daylight. It has been most disturbing."

"The Governor seeks an artifact of your people. A shepherd's staff, hundreds of years old."

"What is its significance?"

"I do not know," replied the soldier. "Our orders are simply to find it and bring it immediately to the Governor."

"I see," Nachum murmured. "Please see to it that I am not disturbed during this search." Nachum spoke with the confidence of a king, knowing his wealth and fame had bought the respect of the army that controlled his people and their land. This was of little matter to him, since Nachum was more Roman than he was Jewish.

"I will send an attendant with you to notify the commander in charge of your area," the soldier responded. The soldier motioned toward one member of the Legion guarding the road. That soldier, in turn, walked back to his commander. The commander gave instructions, and the soldier saluted and immediately mounted a horse tied up nearby. The soldier kicked his horse into action, maneuvering it over to Nachum on his white stallion.

"Please follow me," he said. Both men rode off together, back to the city's center.

Neither spoke as they rode. After many minutes, Nachum finally broke the silence as they entered the complex maze of streets which led into the heart of the city.

"Go on to complete your orders. I must stop to water my horse." The soldier simply nodded, and rode on without saying a word.

Nachum broke off and made a series of turns through the winding roads leading to the city's water source.

*   *   *

High up over the city, Levi had drifted into deep meditative prayer. It was not uncommon for Kabbalists to immerse into a state of deep concentration.

Hoof beats from the courtyard below drew him back to consciousness. Levi carefully unfolded open the window covering and spied below. It was still the middle of the night, but the base of the structure was relatively well lit, as people came for water throughout the night. Even still, the commotion of the night left the courtyard unusually empty. Levi heard the sounds of footsteps walking casually on the wooden base of the cistern. He peeked out the window to see a man on horseback had gotten off and was leading the animal to one of the wooden water repositories. Several of these structures were used to accommodate various needs for both humans and animals. One in particular was set aside for the purpose of filling ritual baths known as mikvahs.

Even in the dim light, Levi knew too well who the man was, for only one person was capable of owning such a prized horse. He reflected on the animal and the circumstances in which Nachum came to acquire it. He concluded that if the evening's pogrom continued into the daytime, Nachum possessed the necessary influence to cross the line of soldiers that encircled the city. This freedom allowed Nachum to get his wares to the wealthier Romans on the other side of the city limits, and providence quickly helped Levi realize what needed to happen. Unbeknownst to him, Nachum was to be the Staff's exit out of the city and on its way to its new resting place.   Emotions of relief softened Levi's tightened face.

He worked his way back to the storeroom door. As he inched it open, he leaned his right ear near to the opening. He feared that any noise he made, no matter how faint, would echo down into the courtyard and compromise his covert position. He knew he had to make it down the stairs before the horse was finished drinking. Swiftly and quietly Levi raced downward towards the base of the stairs. Once at the bottom, he camouflaged the Staff amongst a stack of cistern tools, leaving it well hidden. Then, just as the horse pulled away from the water, Levi covered his face with his shawl and approached Nachum from behind.

Levi spoke in an anguished tone. "Beg your pardon, my master, but could you help a poor beggar?"

"Get away from me you dirty thing," Nachum replied in a nasty tone as he climbed back onto his horse. The animal was finished drinking.

"If it would please my master, I know my master's trade," Levi continued. "Perhaps for a meal I could polish and prepare my master's wares for his day in the morrow's market? I know it is late, but the night is filled with suffering, and I am certain to go hungry until the soldiers find what they seek."

"You are willing to prepare my wares for tomorrow's market?" Nachum questioned. "Just for some food? What else is it you want in return?"

"Only a day's worth of food and a small spot in your barn to rest until we are ready to take your wares to the city. Once there, I will help you unpack your wagon and then I will go away."

Nachum loved the control he held over his people. His massive ego blinded his logic as he did not even bother to question Levi as to who he was, or what he was doing walking the streets and not hiding from the Roman insurgence. "Alright," he responded in a controlling tone, "follow me."

Nachum turned his horse in the direction of his home and proceeded down the alleyway. Levi reluctantly followed Nachum, looking back towards the Staff, seeing it bundled together with the old tools. He prayed that the obvious would be overlooked should the soldiers return before he could retrieve it. There was no other way.

5

As expected, the Roman commander received word to leave Nachum's home untouched. Nachum arrived with Levi hurrying but still trailing ten paces behind. Nachum led his horse into the large stable that adjoined his home. Levi entered behind him and looked around. Even for a stable, it was lavishly supplied. On one side stood the wood and metal wagon that transported the day's supplies. Next to it were crates filled with metal wares of all shapes and sizes, qualities and purposes. They were mostly made out of copper and iron. The affluent were the purchasers of these goods since the cost to acquire was prohibitive for the masses. There were mixing bowls, plates, pitchers, and other common household goods. Thrown about here and there were tools, craftsmen's supplies, and a myriad of trinkets. Nachum had paid little for these items that became his inventory. He had a knack for taking advantage of other's desperation, oftentimes bringing home an entire wagon filled with inventory simply for the price of a day's worth of food.

"Those five crates there are my supply for tomorrow's day at the market," he explained, pointing to the wooden boxes. "Everything in them needs to be in satisfactory shape by morning. I want them polished and shiny. I don't want to see one fingerprint on them."

"I see that they are already of very fine quality," Levi observed. "Already in shape for a good price."

"Then make them in shape for a better price," Nachum retorted. "Do you expect payment for no work?"

Levi expected no less from Nachum, "Very well, my master. You are indeed kind to your servant."

Nachum could never hear those words enough, for he actually believed he *was* a good man.

"If I have found favor in your eyes, please let your servant return to his home, in order that I return with a small sack of needs for tomorrow's work. I assure you, the work required for tomorrow shall be completed to your liking."

Still smiling through his thin lips, Nachum replied boorishly, "Very well. But you *must* return within ten minutes, or I close the barn. I cannot be expected to wait up for you any longer than it takes me to prepare for bed."

"It is understood, my master. I shall return in ten minutes and no more." With that, Levi turned and raced back to the cistern to retrieve the Staff, all the while praying for it to still be where he hid it. He prayed as well for the strength and knowledge essential to ready Nachum's merchandise for market the next morning, to carry out the holy plan.

Levi arrived back at the cistern to find a group of Roman soldiers working their way through the various alleyways situated not far from the structure's entrance. The soldiers were engaged in their search of nearby homes, much to the dismay of their owners. In order to be where Levi saw them, the soldiers must have walked by the staircase and the hoard of tools that stood nearby. Levi stopped and hid against a wall, waiting for the Romans to work their search deeper into the alleyway, moving further away from the cistern. The waiting was painful. Levi's precious minutes seemed to burn by quickly.

Once he felt it safe enough to do so, Levi carefully crept toward the tools. A sigh of relief escaped his lips once he confirmed the Staff still stood covered by the shroud amongst the tools where he had hidden it. Levi had gambled the soldiers would overlook the hasty disguise and won! Knowing the area was empty of people, he reached into the pile and retrieved the Staff. Once he held it in his hands again, he immediately turned and raced back to Nachum's house before the miser grew restless. During his route he gave thanks and prayed for forgiveness for putting the Staff at risk of discovery. The stress of the last few hours was taking its toll as he debated whether leaving the Staff out in the open was a plan from Heaven or his risky but effective idea.

Levi was relieved when he arrived at Nachum's stable on time and without incident. Never could he have dreamt in a million years he would actually be *glad* to be in Nachum's stable! *Life's ironies*, he marveled to himself, amazed at the Almighty's plan of hiding the Staff with an impure vessel such as Nachum... and what's more, in the degenerate's *own* stable! The lights were immediately extinguished in the house when Nachum learned Levi had returned.

*   *   *

Left alone and safe inside the stable, Levi went right to work. He walked over to five filled crates that were adjacent to the empty wagon. The wagon was covered with canvas tarps that lay waiting to be used as protective covers for the crates during transport. He spotted some old rags on an old wooden shelf that was attached to the wall on the opposite side of the barn. Underneath the shelf some closed clay pots were scattered on the dirt floor. Levi walked over to the shelf and took a rag from the top of the pile. He then lifted a lid from one of the pots, affirming it contained polish needed for the metal utensils. He doused a rag with a small amount of the liquid and returned to the crates. He rubbed the liquid filled rag all over the first item from the crate- a copper soup ladle. After a few minutes of rubbing its bottom, the ladle began to reflect a clear, concave reflection of the stable's burning oil lamps which hung from the front wall of the stable. Levi placed an empty crate on the wagon and carefully wrapped the soup ladle and placed it into the crate. Then he started the arduous task of applying the same care to each of the remaining items lying in the five crates.

A long evening awaited an already physically and mentally exhausted Levi. Piece by piece, hour by hour, Levi filled the wagon with polished copper and ironware. Crying as he polished, he dwelled on the wonder if the Romans had found his father and the rest of his family. What was their fate? Were his sister and sisters-in-law defiled in front of their children? Were his brothers killed? The angst of the unknown hurt him to the core, but he continued polishing, knowing he must do his part to carry out God's plan.

Hours later, Levi finished the last piece of the last crate as the sun began its crest on the horizon. Levi looked at all he had done. Satisfied with his workmanship, he collapsed in a heap in a corner of the barn on the dirt floor.

*　　*　　*

A blast of sunlight pierced the barn, its doors opened with a discourteous blow.

"Time for the market!" yelled Nachum as he saw Levi curled up in a fetal position. At first, Nachum considered punishing Levi for sleeping, but when he saw his wagon filled, covered, tied and thoroughly prepared for departure, his anger abated.

Levi had managed to sleep a little over thirty minutes. His head pounded from exhaustion, his mouth was dry from dehydration, and his entire body hurt from the last twelve hours of tension and fear. In one lucid moment, he thought of his Abba- his father. Levi's quick prayer was that his father had mercifully been discovered by his siblings; not the Romans, who would have stopped at nothing to set the house on fire as well as the old man in their ruthless search for the Staff.

As he stood up, Levi discreetly glanced at the wagon filled with Nachum's wares for the market. Looking through the space between two wooden slats that made up the wagon bed, he could barely make out the concealed Staff, lying well hidden and securely attached to the bottom of the wagon.

"Saddle the horse and attach the wagon to him. We will leave as soon as I relieve myself." Nachum walked away and turned the corner to an adjacent alleyway. Levi was disgusted at Nachum's careless choice of locations for doing so. He prepared the horse for riding and attached the wagon to the harness of the saddle as he was ordered. Moments later Nachum returned and mounted his horse, pleased by the good work Levi had done. Gently kicking the horse's side as the signal to move, Nachum rode ahead with Levi following behind.

Nachum, Levi, the horse and the wagon zigzagged through the old city's maze of streets. No words were exchanged between the men. A while later Nachum finally broke the silence.

Nachum turned around to look at Levi. "You are a devout man," Nachum observed out loud. "But with all your devotion, look how you walk! So low and desolate! I on the other hand, who have no need for your books and rituals, have made a life that men would kill for. Who is truly better off- you or me?"

"This world is but the entryway to the palace," Levi retorted. "You have chosen to enjoy this world of existence, and I have chosen to save my enjoyment for the next world which will be far more pleasurable and permanent."

Nachum stared at Levi, not knowing what to make of his curious statement.

After a while, the group made it to the same checkpoint Nachum had been at the night before. A long line of merchants waited helplessly as every wagon, person, and crate was searched by the Roman guards for the Staff. Nachum brashly strode past the long line to the front. Even though these were a different set of soldiers from the previous night, Nachum was not a stranger to them. He motioned to the guards, who walked over to Nachum's wagon like dogs to their master at feeding time.

"For your troubles my lords," Nachum greeted the soldiers as he handed them each a sparkling gold coin. I've got many nice gifts today for your wives. Please do have them stop by for a visit at the market. I assure you I will take good care of them, as honor for your continued patronage."

The soldiers walked away, like children having just received a piece of candy. Nachum, Levi and his horse-drawn wagon walked through the checkpoint; the soldiers completely indifferent to what Nachum carried in his wagon.

When they were safely one hundred yards past the checkpoint, Levi looked toward Heaven and gave thanks to The Creator.

6

Sunlight was now in great abundance over the eastern sky. It had been a half-hour since the duo and horse-drawn wagon had passed the Roman checkpoint. Not a word had been uttered between the two men, as each was deeply engrossed in thought. Nachum, perched on his horse, lost himself on thoughts of his business and material things. Trailing behind on foot, Levi meditated in his morning prayers. His thoughts then turned to reflect back on all that had happened over the last half day. The painful image of his dying father still haunted him. Levi couldn't help but worry over who had found the sage, not to mention what would be done with him after that.

A few hundred yards to the north was one of the main entrances to the walled portion of the city. Levi, Nachum and the wagon were just outside the most affluent neighborhood of Jerusalem. Large, well-built houses constructed of Jerusalem Stone were uniformly stacked against one another forming a beautiful sea of golden uniformity that gave the city its reputation as the most beautiful of its time. Each home contained at least four rooms, double and even triple the sizes of ordinary dwellings. Nachum stopped his horse and dismounted. He walked to the side of the road and relieved himself once again. Levi concentrated his view toward the beautiful site now in front of him. The view of the divine city from this vantage point was simply breathtaking. From here, one had a clear view of the Holy Temple and its surroundings. The alter that stood next to the entrance of the Temple and its courtyard was awesome beyond words. Rarely was Levi able to make it to this place. Few opportunities had allowed the young scholar to leave his father, his books, and his studies. But each of the few times that Levi stood here, he was always in awe of the great walled city. Nachum continued to urinate.

Levi happened to glance to his right to see a man standing on the road fifty yards from their position. He hadn't recalled seeing anyone on the road previously; the morning still too young for most travelers to be out so early. Yet the man was there, standing stiff as a statue, his gaze fixed straight at Levi, the horse, and the urinating Nachum, all-the-while holding out his left arm parallel to the ground and pointing eastward. At first, Levi was worried the man was a Roman soldier, and that Nachum's current activity had angered him. But the man was not wearing a uniform of any sort; rather, he wore the clothing of a common Jewish citizen. Though it was not unusual for the Romans to dress undercover to spy on the Jews, this man did not conduct himself as a soldier surely would have by now. Rather, the man stood in the middle of the road staring, with his arm remaining extended and pointing to the east like a compass.

"Perhaps this man is angry that Nachum is desecrating the holy city by doing what he is doing," Levi thought to himself. He studied the man and his unusual behavior; only to have his concentration broken by Nachum, already back atop his horse, yelling for the young Kabbalist to get moving. Levi followed the horse and wagon and continued down the road. They walked straight toward the strange man.

Levi never took his eyes off the man as he and Nachum slowly made their way down the path that led right to him. When they were closer, Levi could make out the features of the stranger's odd face. His eyes were black like coal and their unblinking, piercing gaze revealed this was no ordinary man. His blank face showed no emotion, no movement- just like the rest of his body. He simply stood in the middle of the dirt road staring... and waiting. The man showed no fear of Nachum, which was most unusual. The stranger did nothing except stand in the middle of the road and stare at them. Levi looked up toward Nachum to see his reaction. Even stranger than the man was the fact that Nachum did not even seem to notice the man at all. To Nachum, it was as if the man did not even exist.

When Nachum's horse finally reached the man, it came to an abrupt halt without being commanded. Surprised at the stallion's bizarre behavior, Nachum kicked his horse on both sides, urging him to continue. Yet, the horse would not move. Nachum pulled out his black leather whip that was fastened to the side harness. He snapped the whip through air to attract the animal's attention. Usually, the horse would have reacted instinctively, but it did not so much as flinch. Nachum snapped the whip once again in the air, this time perfectly placed just above the horse's left ear. Still, the horse did not move. Nachum's anger was rising; his face flushed red, and his lips became puckered and tight. The next use of the whip was more severe as the small leathery end connected with the horse at the most sensitive area on the back of his head. The helpless animal let out a shriek of pain. Still, this was not enough to get the stallion to move. For all the pain it endured, the horse maintained its position, steadfast in front of the man, moving no closer to him.

Levi stood as a helpless witness to the events. Any means of intervention would guarantee equal treatment. Nachum got off the horse, repetitively striking the poor animal without mercy. The stallion stood perfectly still as blood rolled down its outside from several wounds inflicted on its body. It was at this point the unusual stranger spoke. Nachum, however, heard nothing, but Levi perceived his words clearly and the message was unmistakable- this man was Heaven-sent and all that had occurred over the last half day was part of the Eternal Plan.

Without fear, Levi spoke to Nachum. "What has this beast of burden done that you have struck him so wickedly?"

Nachum's anger turned momentarily to bewilderment. No Jew ever had the courage to confront him before. In a flash, Nachum regained his composure and prepared to deliver a reply to Levi's question with a brutal lashing. His arm rose in preparation for the whip to strike Levi in the center of his face. Nachum's arm came down at full speed and the stranger moved, with great agility, right in front of Nachum. The invisible, opposing force had the resistance of a brick wall when Nachum's arm connected with it, and the bones in his lower arm and hand shattered on impact. Nachum screamed out in agony as the whip dropped out of his hand and onto the ground. Nachum fell to the ground, screaming in pain.

Levi stood over Nachum and calmly continued, "Is this beast not your faithful horse that you have ridden all these years?"

Nachum was now lying on the ground, writhing back-and-forth in a fetal position as the surging pain made its crescendo into sheer agony.

7

The immense pain shooting up his arm was more than Nachum could bear. He vomited violently before losing consciousness. Levi looked carefully around for any witnesses to the event. Fortunately, no one was in sight. Levi knew his prayers for the safety of the Staff had been accepted.

The stranger resumed his rigid stance, once again pointing to the east. Levi moved to face him, and with one look, prostrated himself on the ground before the stranger.

"Son of man, do not bow to me." Levi heard the man's voice, but it was not audible.

"But I know what you are." Though instructed to rise, Levi still could not look at the man as he stood. He was too humble to look upon a messenger from the Next World.

"Then you know for what purpose I have been sent," the man replied.

"I do. You are here to guide me to the Staff's new resting place."

"Yes. Man does not yet merit the ability to reveal the Staff and so it must be hidden once again. It is because of this that your father asked that you become the agent to complete his mission."

"My father?! How could that be? He died yesterday! How could he have told you?"

"He is here now."

Levi collapsed to his knees as he suddenly felt the presence of his father's soul embracing him. He buried his face in his hands, searching within for the strength he would surely need to complete the quest.

"Be strong, son of man. And go. Go east toward the entrance to the Judean desert. The knowledge needed to safely deliver the Staff is already within you and all around you. Search your mind and trust your instincts. If you do this, you will surely succeed."

Slowly, Levi resolved to look at the man. But as he lifted his head to behold the stranger, he was gone. Levi blessed the spot where the being stood, acknowledging the exchange as the newest, but not last, pinnacle of his entire life's efforts. He had come face to face with the Divine; he had encountered an angel of God.

*   *   *

Turning toward the horse and wagon, Levi observed that the white stallion no longer stood sternly, but rather had bent his front legs down as a knight would in front of his king. The blood and wounds that had stained his pure coat with crimson had somehow vanished. Levi walked over to the awesome animal which now was bent in submission, awaiting his orders from his new master.

"Get up, my friend," Levi whispered into the horse's ear. "There is no need to bow to me. We were brought together as partners in order to do the will of God." Levi fondly stroked the horse's beautiful white mane. "We have been informed to take an alternative path, and thus should be on our way." Levi walked behind the horse to the cart and crawled underneath it to release the Staff from its secret location. He inspected the Staff through the shroud, as he had continuously maintained his respect for the holy object and never cast his eyes upon it. Assured that the Staff was still secure and unbroken, Levi got up and walked back to the horse to release it from the straps that connected it to the wagon. As the wagon was freed it became back-heavy and the front side shot straight upward, releasing the crates to crash to the ground, spilling all their contents on the ground. Nachum remained unconscious on the side of the road, his cart unattended with his precious inventory haplessly scattered across the road.

Levi returned to the front of the stallion and worked the heavy leather straps that were tied around its neck. A fortune in merchandise now littered the side of the road, but these lavish items would only stay a little while before the next lucky travelers on the road looted the entire collection. The stallion maintained his obeisance, and with no other communication, made it known he awaited for Levi to climb on him, as his new master and friend. With a broad smile, Levi hugged and patted the horse and climbed into the saddle. The horse rose to all fours. Levi did not look back as they strode eastward as they had been instructed by the angel, Staff firmly in hand.

8

Entering the expanse of the Negev Desert was like walking through a portal of time. As a student of the Book, Levi's memory recalled the desert's history and miraculous events, all of which were palpable as he cast his eyes upon the great Negev.

The desert was every bit as solitary as it was immense. Its noiselessness was a comfort during the day and unnerving at night. The near midday sun scorched everything in sight. Vegetation was absent in the desert's sandy hills and rocky terrain. Progress was extremely difficult.

Levi looked down from atop the beautiful white beast, his new companion, as it strained to keep along the narrow makeshift road. Amazingly, the stallion knew precisely where to go. The journey was slow, but steady. Miles of hill and rock lie before them.

Even though Levi had gone with no food or water in over eighteen hours, he felt neither thirst nor hunger. The journey into the great wilderness was Levi's first, and the spiritual height he held due to his mission and surroundings were enough to relieve the need of sustenance. He recalled the great miracle that occurred that enabled him to smuggle the Staff from the Roman Legion, the angel he met on the road and of course, his father.

Hour by hour they treaded onward as his mind's eye imagined all the events that took place in the very place he and the horse came upon. He imagined his ancestors, the great sages of his people as they once occupied this area for spiritual training. In fact, many yeshivas, the schools of religious learning, spiritual meditation and training, were built here and produced great prophets. Only the solitude of a great desert could provide these spiritual souls the environment needed to train to attain the prophetic state.

Sixteen hours after being sent into the desert the rocky road, hot sun and lack of food and water finally began taking its toll on the companions. Levi surveyed the next row of hills ahead. At first glance, they appeared no different than the previous hills with stone-strewn fortresses of dirt and rock, but Levi had a premonition about them. Soon thereafter, Levi began to realize the differences. They were indeed distinct, but not by their physical characteristics. There was something inexplicably special about this location, and Levi knew somewhere in that area was where he needed to go.

Crossing over the rock-laden land atop the white stallion was, at first, extremely labored. Now, it was nearly impossible. The further the man and horse ventured toward the hills the more prohibitive the stones became. The horse staggered; exhausted, thirsty and hungry, and now bleeding from scrapes on all fours. The normally pure, white legs of the stallion were now coated with thick patches of bright red and dull brown blood that oozed and dried from lesions it suffered attempting to navigate the sharp edges of the stones. Levi dismounted from the wary creature as quickly as he could. Moving to face the animal, Levi used his Kabbalistic skills and locked his eyes with those of his companion. Without hesitation, Levi silently blessed the horse, kissed its nose and sent it back to Jerusalem. The horse honorably attempted to resist the order, but after several caresses, the beast turned away. With the neighing of allegiance and sentiment, the stallion bode farewell to his friend and short-time master. Levi watched, Staff in hand, as the beautiful horse retreated with perceptible pain out of the rocky valley to the flatland and back to the road for Jerusalem.

Eventually Levi returned his attention to the menacing walls of endless rock that lay scattered in front of him. No sane individual would ever think to set foot into the newly displayed forest of stone alone. But Levi knew somehow, beyond any shadow of doubt, that somewhere in these unforgiving mountains of sand and stone lie the great resting place of the holy artifact that he held in his hand.

He looked down and stared at the shroud that covered the Staff. *"So plain the Staff must be",* he thought. The temptation to gaze upon the Staff was strong, but he did not look at it.

"My mission is to hide you from this world until it earns your return," Levi said to the Staff compassionately. "So please, grant me pardon from having to treat you so disrespectfully."

Levi looked forward toward the distance. He saw the cliffs of the hills far off in the distance overlooking the valley. The hike in would require more than just physical strength. It would require the endurance of another agonizing day without food and water.

The sun was fading in the western horizon. Levi cleared a small section of ground. He lied on the ground and rested his head on a small, smooth rock. Twilight slowly faded to black as the desert's nocturnal noises began to fill the air. Levi nonetheless closed his eyes as his exhausted mind and body could endure no more. He was asleep in seconds.

*   *   *

Even as the sun slowly rose in the eastern sky, the dry heat was relentless. Levi awoke with his lips parched dry and cracked, his eyes red. And though he managed a bit of sleep he was exhausted. But his determination was unwavering. Every muscle in his body ached. Walking into this part of the Negev desert was difficult enough, even for one prepared for such a venture, but the last two days of Levi's life had not permitted such provisions. The absence of necessities in this hostile environment would have spelled death to most, but the encounter with Heaven's messenger prodded Levi forward, for he knew he would be able to execute his mission. Thoughts of his own demise were eventually extinguished the more he meditated on the encounter with the Divine. Nothing of this world, he felt, could instigate fear within him- not even the Romans. In spite of this, he was admittedly growing weaker. The possibility had set in that, though he may succeed in hiding the Staff, the cost of doing so would be to die in the process. But this too he accepted for he knew it would be for the good of his soul. What few character flaws he possessed were slowly being cleansed as he painfully put one foot in front of the other in order to continue forward. Each painful step to the Staff's new place of rest would assuredly increase his spiritual purification. Like the sweating of poison from the body, so too were his sins slowly and painfully drawn from his soul.

Hours passed. Levi looked around. Everything was beginning to look the same. Fatigue had taken its toll. He was no longer able to differentiate between one hill and the next. Every rock appeared like every other rock. There was no distinct path to gain any bearings. He walked in a direction without really knowing if he was simply meandering in circles. He treaded forward, praying he was still on course. The hills shouted back with deafening silence and his ears rang in pain. The sun continued to beat against his back. He had nothing left.

"I feel like I am failing! What have I left undone?" Levi lied down still embracing the holy Staff like a child to its mother, and convulsed with dry tears. It was then that the piercing silence of the lonesome desert was broken by the soothing sound of a dove cooing.

Levi looked up to find the bird. Surely he had lost control of his senses. He strained to focus on the hill opposite where he lay. Convinced the exertion of the last few days had finally robbed him of his faculties, Levi saw a magnificent, pristine, white dove sitting atop a glistening sapphire boulder just above him. It cooed with echoes of love as its song played into the ears of the half-dead righteous man. Yet, as weak as he was, Levi's mind and soul were shook awake again. Whatever feelings that had clouded his mind, Levi's revived will pushed away. Clarity had regained itself. Levi suddenly felt as strong as a lion and raced up the hill for a better look at this beautiful bird.

Natural instinct for most creatures is to flee when any son of man comes their way, but the pure white dove sat calmly; waiting, expecting. The boulder it was perched on was made from material not previously known to the physical world. The bluish crystal surface of the half-ton rock glistened like a recently buffed gem. With his right hand, Levi carefully traced over the polished surface of the stone.

In his left hand, he held the Staff. The surge of ecstasy consumed him like a blazing fire. With the miraculous strength of a dozen men, Levi pushed the rock and moved it three feet to the right, revealing a small opening about two feet wide leading into the mountain. Without hesitation, Levi entered the cave.

Except for the light that came from its opening, the cave was pitch black. Even so, Levi did not need light. He could picture in his mind the cave's layout, perfectly clear. He crawled about, never faltering, as a blind man in his own home, knowing the cave was completely empty, except for the Staff and himself. Four yards from his present position was a cleft in the rock, like a mantle of a fireplace. Fighting off fatigue, Levi held the Staff level in both hands, palms upward while clutching the holy object. Levi knelt down, wearily, in front of the cleft of rock. Tears rolled down his cheeks, as he carefully straightened out the shroud that encased the Staff as a loving father would for his baby, and gently placed it on the cleft. His sobbing was uncontrollable as he sat next to it.

"Master of the World!" he cried, "On behalf of man, I am sorry we have not merited your redemption," he continue to wail, "I am sorry we have not merited your redemption. I am sorry we have not merited your redemption!"

Levi was no longer in control of his emotions. Over and over again he cried for forgiveness. In doing so, he ascended to a new spiritual height, and Levi knew that he had succeeded in his mission of keeping the Staff from evil. God was indeed with him. The Staff was safe, and because of this, he knew it was time to leave the world behind. It would be impossible now for him to return to the world of man. Laying there next to the Staff, Levi closed his eyes, and like his holy father two days ago, he too said the Shmah, the statement of the Jews declaring that God is One and Indivisible. Levi departed this world with a face of contentment and with that, he joined his parents in the Next World.

*   *   *

Outside the cave, in the perfectly still and fiery-hot air of the Negev Desert, not a sound was made. The Earth stood as the sole witness to the event, and acknowledged as such without even a twig snapping. Seconds later, the mountain shook ferociously. The beautiful white dove perched atop the perfectly hewn jewel-stone flew from its perch on the sapphire rock. The mountain shook with fervor, and the jewel-stone, as if being directed, lightly rolled back to its original position. Slowly it turned from the beautiful radiant blue sapphire, to a dull and dusty boulder, no different than the millions of rocks that surrounded it. As a sign, six square inches of the spiritual material was left untouched at the base of the stone, and it glistened in the remaining sunlight of the day... and it repeated this every day for next two thousand years.

9
The Vatican, Rome
May, 2012 A.D.

"I've found some items I would like to look at in private," was the request to the curator.

"Certainly Mr. Pandseh," replied the curator. "The private viewing room has been prepared for you as usual. I will return in two hours to check on your status. Please feel free to contact me via that telephone on the wall should you need anything in the meantime."

"I will. Thank you," Mohsen replied, mostly ignoring the curator's good will. He was eager to have some privacy in the viewing room. The curator closed the doors after him, and Mohsen was finally alone in the vaults.

The secret antiquity vaults of the Vatican are inaccessible to most barring a select few. Their existence however, is really no secret. Many speculate on what is kept in them, but for the masses with an immense interest in relics of historic value, admission to these private areas is merely a dream. It has been said that, among other things, some items contained within the secret vaults contain information that could change the religious balance of power, thus the reason for their secrecy. Entrance is forbidden to even those ruling elite in the Vatican who would otherwise have high clearance to any other area of Vatican City. Authorization to the depository was solely granted by the Pope himself or a trusted few. And when a pope died, those who had been previously allowed could find themselves suddenly forbidden with the appointment of a successor. Mohsen Pandseh had come to them for years, which spoke volumes for the degree of influence he carried not just from one pope, but from *three*. He was not only privy of the vault's location; he knew what was in them, as he had been inside them many times.

Iranian by birth with a strong nationality, Mohsen achieved wealth and status from his involvement with the Iranian government. He was not a direct member of the government, since he wasn't particularly religious, a requirement since the revolution. Rather, he was a businessman who did *favors* for government officials. In his early twenties he created opportunities for himself by providing contraband to government officials when the government instituted a ban on any product deemed too secular for the new religious state created from the revolution and the return of Ayatollah Khomeini from exile. As he grew into his thirties, so did his business.

In fact, his tremendous ascendancy not only afforded him influence within Iran, but throughout the rest of the world.

Though not religious, Mohsen was still passionate about history, particularly religious history. Judaism and Christianity intrigued him from an historical perspective; he studied both Latin and Biblical Hebrew during his days at the university. His education enabled him to thoroughly enjoy his visits to the Vatican's vaults, as the shelves came alive with writings of the ancient ways, providing images of daily life and the challenges they faced, specific to their time. To Mohsen, the problems of the past were *real* problems, as opposed to the trivial issues of today's young adults.

His latest business venture was an importer of lavish and rare items of the world. An illustrious and romantic enterprise that to most was a dream, Mohsen traveled the world in his private jet regularly. Above all valuables, however, was the lucrative business of religious texts and artifacts. There were many believers in the world, and many paid handsomely for otherwise worthless parchments, slips of paper or old books simply because they had a religious tone, or that they came from the secret vaults or an archeological site. For time immemorial, the world was fixated on the Divine and Mohsen took full financial advantage of the faiths of the world.

The Vatican allowed Mohsen to purchase a select number of such documents, which he turned around and sold, earning him a respectable profit in the world's religious artifacts market.

Mohsen was excited for this particular visit, as a certain book he had seen on the shelf previously had aroused his curiosity. The book was not much different at first glance than the hundreds of others that had amassed in these secret chambers. This book, however, lacked any writing whatsoever on the cover. No preceding book lacked an author's name or at least its title. Thus, he knew exactly what he wanted to see on this trip, and it was the first of only three books he bothered to retrieve from the archives.

Mohsen stood in the private viewing room and anxiously put on the necessary garments required for examining artifacts; surgeon's gloves and cap. The entire antiquities vault, including its viewing rooms, had humidity control, much like a cigar humidor. Sweating was therefore common place necessitating a head covering as well. Mohsen carefully opened the small, parched, leather-bound cover. Scanning the first few pages revealed nothing more than the author's notes. Mohsen's moderate fluency in Hebrew showed this book to be a work from roughly the first century, A.D. That knowledge always provided a spark of excitement and adrenaline since not many books of that era survived the book burnings by various world and religious powers over the centuries, intending to forever dispose of the heretical information found in them. In fact, ninety-five percent of all documents that survived were locked away in the very vaults to which Mohsen had open access.

Tremendous anxiousness mounted within as he continued thumbing through the pages, hoping to find something more substantial. After skimming a large portion of the book, the excitement and adrenaline wore off, as Mohsen saw nothing more than a Hebrew scholar's thoughts jotted down on parchment. Disappointment overcame him as Mohsen set the book aside.

"No wonder there was no writing on the cover," the frustrated millionaire thought. Just as he was about to move his attention from this curious book a little piece of parchment barely jutting out of its corner caught his eye. He carefully opened the book to the page where the parchment was loosely held. A small piece of vellum, roughly four inches square was folded in half and tucked in the crease between the pages. Small Hebrew letters could be seen from the opposite side of the thin paper. Though kept as moist as possible, the parchment was extremely dry and Mohsen was concerned if opened, it may crack. Knowing this, he promptly turned on the warm, moist air of the table humidifier that was placed on the viewing desk. The humid air gently streamed over the tabletop. Mohsen delicately took the folded paper with special tweezers and held it straight into the oncoming stream of humid air. Steadily, he held the paper in the fine mist of the air for nearly seven minutes, alternating his grip on the tweezers between his right and left hands to keep the tension from causing a cramp. Mohsen finally saw the paper becoming flexible enough to unfold.

"Just a little longer to be sure," Mohsen breathed to himself in anticipation. Without looking, he grabbed another set of tweezers from the table with his free hand and locked them onto a corner of the parchment. With the dexterity of a surgeon, Mohsen painstakingly unfolded the paper. Years of storing the book in this humid environment had paid off, as the ink lettering did not crumble upon unfolding the paper. The paper was now fully open and, with the exception of some minor cracking of the ink around the letters, the contents were clear and legible. The text was written in ancient Ashurit Hebrew script.

His moderate fluency proved sufficient, as Mohsen stumbled through the flow of words. The message seemed to be about a man relaying a dream, and the dream revealed the location of the 'Matei Moshe', The Holy Staff of Moses.

10
Denver, CO
May, 2012

Glenn had only been back in Denver for a week and was bored already. Drinking a beer and doodling on his electronic keyboard in his room at his parent's house, he thought about last week in New York and how much he couldn't wait to get out of there. The city's frantic pace was taking its toll on him. Glenn had hoped his return to a slower paced Denver would provide a creative spark for a new album. He figured a quieter environment back home would ease his mind and the inspiration he sought would flow, but that hadn't happened yet.

Glenn was a very talented musician. He formed a band when he was a sophomore in high-school, and performed at school functions and private parties. Handsome and talented, he had no shortage of girlfriends. He knew how to play the crowd when he performed and for that, never left a gig without a girl by his side. He loved making music and subsequently made the commitment to dedicate the next few years after high-school to do it professionally. At the time, Manhattan afforded the best opportunity for his musical talents to become noticed.

Two years had passed since he moved from Denver to his little studio in SoHo. Expensive wasn't the word to describe the cost of living there. Rent alone left him little for anything else, even though he was working full-time in addition to performing four to five nights a week. His was living in the classic 'poor musician's world; work your ass off in a mindless job during the day, play gigs at night, and burn out in the process.

Thoughts of returning to New York were interrupted when he looked out from his old bedroom window on the second floor to watch the sun setting behind the Rocky Mountains. His folks had a place in the southeast part of town, on the top of a small hill. The hill was small, but still high enough for their home to have an unhindered view of the mountains. As the sun set, a cloud layer hovering over the west erupted into a breathtaking burst of red, orange and purple fire.

While looking at the incredible light show nature was performing for him, he acknowledged his creativity, or lack thereof, was the result of his psychological state and not necessarily his physical environment. A week of doing nothing but waiting for his muse passed, when a glimpse of a song teased his mind. However, every time he tried to put it to paper, frustration returned as the idea vanished. Casting his lot to the wind and admitting his writer's block, he tried to let go of the self-imposed pressure. *"Everything in its own time. The creativity will flow... just give it time,"* he thought. The doorbell rang downstairs interrupting his drifting thoughts. He opened his bedroom door and shuffled down the stairs to answer when he heard his mom had already beat him to the front door.

"Chayim!" his mom cried with delight from the open doorway.

Glenn's best friend from childhood, Howard, or Chayim as he now requested to be called, was also in town. Coincidently, he had just arrived back in Denver from New Jersey where he was a student in a religious seminary known as a yeshiva. The yeshiva had just concluded its studies for the semester and Howard had flown back to Denver to spend an indefinite period of time at home keeping his mother company. Howard had always been religious growing up, and his spiritual journey took him to the day schools of Lakewood, New Jersey. The yeshiva boasted the highest enrollment of students in the world; over three thousand students. There, Howard began to use his Hebrew name given to him at birth- Chayim. Both Glenn's and Chayim's families still lived in the same houses from their childhoods, across the street from one another. Glenn and Chayim had been friends since either could remember. Both of their mothers each told them they were so much alike, they were considered twin sons of different mothers.

"Hello Mrs. Z," a very different looking Chayim replied from the doorway. The old Howard dressed in jeans and a t-shirt. The new Chayim now stood there wearing a black suit, white shirt with a silver patterned tie loosely tied, a black hat and a long, scraggly beard. Glenn's mom made the customary move to give Chayim and kiss and hug, but was met with a step backward to keep them from touching.

"Oh crap," Mrs. Zall blurted as she remembered the orthodox Jewish restriction of men and women touching. "This no touching stuff has to include *me* too? You're like my own son!"

"Sorry mom," Chayim replied with a smirk on his face. "Rules are rules. How are you doing?"

"We're all fine here. How's your mom doing?" Mrs. Zall asked as her faced changed from happy to one of concern. Though they lived across the street, there was not much interaction between the two women. Chayim's father had passed away two days after Christmas, six months prior.

"She's depressed. Which is why I decided to come home for the summer," Chayim said.

"I'd ask you to give her a kiss for me, but I know that's not going to happen!" Mrs. Z smiled facetiously. "Glenn's upstairs. I'll..."

"I'm right here Ma," Glenn interjected as he jogged down the staircase. He was smiling ear to ear as he looked at Chayim, standing in the foray. The two young men couldn't have looked any different; Chayim and his black and white garb, religious fringes hanging down underneath his suit coat, black dress hat and long beard; Glenn in faded jeans with a hole in the right knee, t-shirt and bare feet. "Hey dude. How the hell are you?"

"What up?" Chayim replied in a manner becoming of him from his previous life before the yeshiva. The two hugged like brothers, slapping each other on the back.

"Jesus, look at you," Glenn said as he looked Chayim up and down at his yeshiva outfit. You're a regular Holy Roller!"

"Yeah, but I'm still the same old Howie, except you now have to call me Chayim. And yes, I think I'll have a beer, thank you very much," he said with his usual sarcasm, which was well met.

"Why yes, your Holiness, I'll get that right away!" Glenn rebutted with equal sarcasm, as he bowed to Chayim in a servant-like manner. He retreated to the kitchen to grab two bottles of beer from the refrigerator.

"So Howie, how-," Glenn's mother began.

"Chayim."

"Oh God. Howie, this is going to take-."

"Chayim."

"Chayim. This is going to take awhile to get used to. You can't just expect an old dog like me to change just like that, you know."

Chayim began his lecture. "I know what it's like. But you'll get used to it in time. Before you know it, you'll be changing your name too, because you'll see it's so cool! But until then, try and get the C-H part of it down. It's not *Hayim*, with an 'H'. It's *Chayim*- say it like you're clearing your throat. Ccccchhhhayim."

"One miracle at a time, my dear. For now, I have to work on the Howard to Chayim transition. We'll go from there." Glenn's mom smiled as she went back to her office, down the hallway, to return to her work.

Glenn reappeared with two open bottles of Budweiser. "These kosher?" he continued to banter.

"Fuck you and give me one," Chayim responded, with half a smile on his face. The traditional *'Fuck you'* either vocally or by finger was their mutual machismo-style salutation of 'I love you, man' without actually having to say it.

Glenn led Chayim up the stairs to his room, where music was already playing. Glenn motioned for his friend to take a seat in an easy chair located on the left side of the small room. Because of the chair, bed, computer desk, bookshelf and his electronic keyboard, the room was cozily snug.

"Is this CD you?" Chayim asked as he looked around for the CD cover trying to identify the artist currently playing.

"Yep," Glenn sighed, reclining on his bed. Speakers surrounded the bedroom at all four corners, playing some nice, soft jazz. Nothing had changed here in ten years. To Chayim, it was like entering a time capsule whenever he walked in it. All the memories- good, bad, and ugly- always poured through him in the first few minutes after walking in.

Glenn continued. "It's the album we put together about two years ago, but it never got released. I thought it was great work, but I couldn't get my producer to accept it for production. He said some bullshit about it all sounding like my other stuff, and that he wanted something *different* this time around. So now I'm on a timeline to come up with something 'new', and I'm drawing a total blank. This has been going on six weeks now. And, to make it worse I'm starting to look at the timeline, and it's giving me shpilkes. So, here I am, back in Denver *'trying to get that feeling again'* as Barry Manilow puts it. I thought that a little time out of New York would be good for me, but now I'm thinking that that isn't true. The only thing that's certain is that I've got a mental block, and being back in Denver hasn't helped it go away. To make it worse, this vicious cycle of being under a deadline makes my mind go blank, and the more it does, the closer the deadline gets, which makes my mind go blank, and blah blah blah. Long story short, I'm listening to this album to see if I can figure out why my producer thinks it's the same ol' same ol'. Maybe that'll get me going in the right direction again."

Chayim was already halfway done with his beer. "It sounds great to me, and a lot different than what I heard on the last CD you sent me."

"Thanks dude. I wish you were my producer saying that. I'm really starting to get sick of that guy. I've got one more album with him and then my contract's up. I'm thinking I can do better with someone else. The problem is, he's got a lot, and I mean a *lot* of contacts in the field. He's got the power to make or break you. And he knows it too, the assbite." Glenn took a big swig from his beer.

"Well, I'm glad you're here," Chayim said before taking another drink. "I've been coming in a lot to see my mom since my dad died. And, even though she loves it, it's starting to drive me crazy. But what can I do? I can't expect her to carry on with her life in just six months. Seeing my dad every day for twenty-five years and then 'poof' one day he's gone. It has to be quite an adjustment."

"She okay?" Glenn asked. He admitted to himself that his problem was small in comparison to what Chayim and his mom were going through. But he also took comfort knowing someone else had problems too. He already knew that, but it felt good to hear it although he didn't tell Chayim that. Their short conversation had Glenn feeling a bit of the pressure of *his* problem subsiding a little, and in such a short period of time. It was good to have Chayim for some companionship, he was thinking as they talked.

"She's a whole lot stronger than I gave her credit for. But me being so far away makes things harder. She's so happy when I come home, but a total basket case on the day I leave. It's almost not worth coming in. But for sure the good outweighs the bad. So, here I am, once again." It was Chayim's turn to take a big swig of beer.

"How long are you in for?"

"Don't know yet. I'll see how long it goes before my brain says, 'time to go'. Besides, I can always do my work from here. Learning can be done anywhere on the planet. That's the up side to my life. It doesn't pay worth a damn, but the spiritual insight is the best."

"I give you a lot of credit How-, er, I mean Chayim, for this new life of yours," Glenn said. "I, for one, understand the quest for a higher reality. We always knew the pot-smoking we did as kids would lead to stronger stuff. I just never knew it would be in the form of a black skullcap and fringes."

"Don't worry," Chayim retorted. "You'll be joining me at the yeshiva before you know it."

"Fat chance. I find spirituality through my music."

"What?" Chayim responded incredulously. "Do you know how many musicians are enrolled in the yeshiva? There must be at least two hundred! And some of the tunes they come up with are used during prayer. You talk about spiritual!"

Glenn was lying on his bed staring at the ceiling. It was obvious that Chayim had struck a note, as he momentarily questioned his preconceived ideas of living a religious life.

Comfortable silence filled the air as both young men drifted into their own thoughts as Glenn's music continued to play in the background. The ambiance from the compositions produced an aura of mystery in the room.

Chayim jumped enthusiastically off of the chair when he looked up at Glenn's bookshelf. Surprisingly, Glenn still had his Old Testament that was given to him for his bar-mitzvah. Chayim pulled the thick book from the shelf and began thumbing through the pages. Glenn remained passive, still lying on his bed, drinking his beer.

"I want to show you something from the Torah. Don't worry, I'm not trying to turn you into a religious fanatic. I just want you to see some of the things that make me think and believe the way I do. Maybe just like you feel when you've got that special feeling, when you're onto a new song. There's a flame within me that ignites when I see some of these passages." Chayim flipped to the first chapter of the Old Testament, 'Genesis'.

"Check *this* out. In the very first few lines of the Bible, line three to be specific, it says, 'God said, 'Let there be light, and there was light.' Then line five says, 'God called to the light: "Day" and to the darkness He called "Night". And there was evening and morning, one day.'"

"See Chayim," said Glenn argumentively, "that's all fine and dandy, but I don't think that-"

"Let me finish," Chayim interrupted. Glenn was irritated that Chayim cut him off. It was never Chayim's nature to do that.

"So, as I was saying, God created 'light' on the first day of creation. But let me ask you a question. What day were the sun and moon created?"

Glenn stared blankly for a few seconds. He shrugged his shoulders and raised his eyebrows with no answer to offer.

"They were created on the *fourth* day, Glenn. So tell me, what is this 'light' that was created on the first day, if the sun wasn't created until the fourth?"

Chayim returned Glenn's perplexed gaze with a manner of conviction. "The sages explain in detail what the light is, but the bottom line is, that the light created on the first day wasn't light from the sun, it was a special 'spiritual' light.

Glenn stared at Chayim without blinking, without emotion. After a long silence, Glenn replied, "That's fucking spiritual."

Chayim smiled back at Glenn's manner of reply. "Yeah, it sure is." Then he took another drink and finished his beer.

Chayim sat back on the chair again with the book. Neither said a word. The CD changer flipped to another CD. This time it was the New Age group 'Tangerine Dream' that was playing. Glenn broke the silence.

"Give me one more of those little quips."

Chayim considered the request for a moment. "Okay, here's one that is brought up not only in yeshivas but in top universities too. Most scientists are pretty much in agreement that the age of the universe is roughly fifteen billion years old. They chuckle at Judaism's calendar since it claims that the time since creation is only a little over five thousand seven hundred and sixty years. For years science and religion have clashed and this discrepancy is a fundamental example of their differences. In the first chapter of Genesis, specifically the first six days of creation, *before* man's creation which occurred on the sixth day, whenever we read *'And there was evening and there was morning,'*- we actually don't know how *long* these 'days' were. Since God lives outside of time, these 'days' are 'God' days, whatever that means, and these 'days' could be billions of years for all we know. So, according to Kabbalah, the six thousand years of creation and the fifteen billion years science thinks is the age of the Universe are one and the same, and they're *both* right. Some very bright minds in 'secular' institutions are actually thinking along these ways and becoming very observant and spiritual people in the process.

"The Old Testament and other Judaic texts are filled with these kinds of golden nuggets!" exclaimed Chayim. "All you have to do is open the books and get them for yourself, but hardly anyone ever does."

"I know," Glenn replied, "and I'm one of them. You know how my family feels about religion, Chayim. My dad doesn't care whether God exists or not. What matters to him is getting into a good school and finding a good job after that. Money is the pathway to happiness. God, in his mind, is for the weak and lazy. He said that the clergy are the luckiest people in the world. They are able to live nicely on their congregant's fear of the afterlife."

Silence once again filled the air. After a few moments, Chayim felt compelled to ask, "So do you think your dad is right about all that?" He almost didn't want to hear the answer, for a 'Yes' would mean that Glenn believed Chayim's life passion of studying metaphysics was an exercise for the weak.

Glenn got up from his bed and stared out the window. The awesome sunset he looked at earlier was all but gone and twilight was in its place. He continued, "My dad's a smart guy. But I just don't see how a bright guy like that can be so stupid. How could he possibly think that if you don't have money you're not happy? Most of my parent's friends have cash, yet they or their kids are some of the most miserable and screwed up people I've ever met."

Chayim sighed with relief, chuckling from Glenn's response.

Glenn continued, "You may not believe this Chayim, but I think the stuff you study about is actually pretty cool. But I love my music more. That's just the way it is. But show me one more!"

Chayim mused at the mental image of Glenn becoming a religious scholar, growing out his sideburns and wearing the traditional long black frock found in many ultra-orthodox communities.

"Okay, here's one that I'm actually looking at myself. It's a heavy one, but I think you'll appreciate it."

Glenn went back to his bed a sat forward attentively. He looked like a little kid waiting to hear his bedtime story.

Chayim started, "My Rosh Yeshiva had a dream the-"

"Your *what*?" Glenn broke in.

"Oops, sorry," said Chayim as he remembered who his audience was. "The head of our yeshiva, the principal, is called the 'Rosh Yeshiva'. Rosh is Hebrew for 'head'. So, Rosh Yeshiva means 'Head of the Yeshiva', or 'Head of the Seminary'. Anyway, as I was saying, our Rosh Yeshiva, who I might add is one of the world's authorities in Kabbalah, had a dream about two months ago. He told our class about it, because it was so intense for him. I think it actually scared him. In the dream, he found himself in a beautiful garden. The garden was so beautiful; he knew he had been given the merit of visiting the actual Garden of Eden. Anyway, he gazed at the most stunning plants and trees that he'd ever seen. And the fruit from these trees! Man, our Rosh Yeshiva stared out over our heads as he spoke about his dream- he wanted so much to be back there, it was obvious. 'The Tree' he said, over and over. Tears started to flow. Then he continued while his eyes were still all watery. He said he was walking through the Garden when he saw the first woman. Eve! Standing alone, just after being created from Adam's side, no more than twenty feet away. And how beautiful she was! The second of the only two human beings created by God himself. Even for our Rosh Yeshiva, Eve's beauty was too great to look away from. But his euphoria of being in the Garden of Eden and seeing Eve quickly turned to one of fear and uncertainty. The Rosh Yeshiva said Eve was talking to someone or something and that he wanted to run away from it or scream from sheer terror. What was puzzling was that the object was nothing more than an ordinary shepherd's staff; not the snake that he expected to see. Nevertheless, this object was frightening to look at, but the Rosh Yeshiva couldn't figure out why. Then, in an instant, the dream switched from the famous Garden to the first encounter that Moses had with God."

Glenn was completely riveted. "I know this part! I saw '*The Ten Commandments*'! Moses was standing at the Burning Bush!"

Chayim smirked. Any other time would have made the last sentence amusing, but Glenn was very serious.

Chayim continued. "Right! And what did God tell Moses to do?"

"Pick up the Staff and place it on the ground in front of you. Right?" Chayim was surprised that Glenn actually knew the answer to that question. His friend was completely mesmerized.

"And when Moses laid it down on the ground, it turned into the serpent."

"Yeah, I know that too. So... then what?"

"By this time our Rosh Yeshiva was sitting down and all of us, students and teachers, were circled around him, listening to him intently. For a few of us, this was a first. He totally was reliving two of the all-time fateful events of human history. But, he was still uncertain of the reason. After all, the section of the Old Testament that we were reading for the week had nothing to do with either of these episodes. Anyway, what does the Old Testament say Moses did when the Staff turned into a snake? It says that he ran from it."

Glenn was now more frustrated than curious. He thought he was going to get some big piece of juicy spirituality, but was feeling let down. "Jesus, Chayim, give me a break. What the hell would *you* do if you experienced the same thing? You'd do more than just run from it like Moses did. You'd shit your pants!"

Chayim astutely responded as he would have done before Glenn opened his foul mouth. "Let me ask you something Glenn. If you were Moses, and you're having an audience with the Creator of the entire Universe, you're telling me that you'd be scared of a trick like that? Back to the dream- while Moses ran, my Rosh Yeshiva just stared at the Staff, waiting for something to happen. But then he awoke, as if something was telling him that he'd seen enough. He recited the nullification of a dream, and then-"

Glenn interrupted. "The *what* of a dream?"

"Oh, sorry," Chayim said as he quickly remembered once again he was talking over Glenn's head. "The nullification of a dream. If a person's had a nightmare or a troubling dream, then the next day he recites the nullification in front of three friends. It's basically a prayer asking the dream be only for positive insight and not a forewarning of something bad to come."

"Have *you* ever said it?" Glenn asked.

Chayim shook his head. "I've had so many nightmares since my dad died, that I'd drive my friends crazy each time I needed to."

Glenn recalled that fateful day when he came over to see Chayim, only to find out that his friend had just returned from the hospital where an ambulance had taken his dad after he had a heart attack behind the wheel. His dad had died quickly, and Chayim's life changed forever in a wisp of a moment.

Chayim continued, "So after he nullified the dream, he sought to figure out *why* he was shown the dreams. The Rosh Yeshiva kept telling us over and over again, that he was certain it had to do with the Staff. He told us again how, after Moses ran from it, he remained fixated on the Staff, waiting for something to happen. But nothing ever did."

The two sat silently for a moment. Glenn broke the silence, "But Moses carried the Staff, right? Didn't he split the Red Sea for the Hebrews to cross out of Egypt with it?"

"Right on the money, dude," his friend replied. It was amusing to hear the word "dude" from a guy with the long sideburns and a skullcap. "Check *this* out. You're familiar with King Arthur and the whole Camelot thing, right? King Arthur's magician's name was Merlin. What was *his* source of power? A staff. Do you think that story, and so many like it were mere coincidences? Most folklore has roots in things that are true. The story of Merlin and his magical staff is, according to Kabbalists, an offshoot of the power of the Staff of Moses! Anyway, back to Exodus. If you keep reading, you see that God told Moses to pick up the Staff. Apparently Moses was able to regain his composure and eventually returned to pick it up. But the question of *why* he was afraid of it at the beginning still remains. I believe the Rosh Yeshiva knows the answer but isn't telling us."

"What makes you so sure?"

"Because he's been an *entirely* different person since the episode. He's either nervous or suppressing excitement- I can't tell which. He's on the phone a lot to some people in Israel… but not the religious people you'd expect him to have conversations with. I found out through the grapevine that he's been in touch with the head of the archaeology department at the Hebrew University."

"What do you mean, 'through the grapevine'?" was Glenn's reply tinged with a touch of sarcasm. "You religious guys aren't supposed to gossip!"

No reply was given and Glenn just smiled triumphantly. Chayim rolled his eyes upward.

"*Whatever*." Chayim finally said, trying to come out on top.

"So you're thinking that whatever the dream was about was enough to prompt some sort of unusual reaction on your principal's part?"

"Definitely," said Chayim. "My Rosh Yeshiva's circle of people are definitely not the secular type. In fact, the rabbis and archaeologists are at odds with one another. The rabbis are angry that the archaeologists allow excavation to occur at holy sites. Some of the things that are uncovered, like bodies and stuff, are meant to be left alone. So the contact is highly unusual. In fact, it's downright scary. I know something's going on."

"Well, figure out a way to find out!" Glenn blurted in frustration. It was like he had been drawn into a mystery movie only to find the movie projector fizzle out in the middle of the movie. "This shit's too cool to just say 'Oh gosh, something amazing is going on, but I'm too much of a weenie to figure out what's really going on."

Chayim's training in the yeshiva served him well in this instance. He knew that Glenn was antagonizing him, and the cooler Chayim played, the redder Glenn's face became. Deep down, however, he knew Glenn was right. He was just as curious as anyone to know what was happening, and eventually gave in.

"Alright." Chayim responded after a staring match ensued. "I'll tell you what I'll do. I'll send an email to my Rosh Yeshiva about something completely unrelated. Then, at the end of the email, I'll write that I hope he's feeling better from whatever's been happening, and that if I can do anything to assist, I'd be glad to help. That's really all I can do. You have to understand the teacher-student relationship of the Yeshiva world. I can't go right up to him and offer advice, ask questions about what's wrong, or anything like that. That's just not the way things are done in this system."

"Fine. Okay," Glenn replied, obviously agitated. It seemed when Howie became Chayim, a lot more than his name changed. The black hat world of the Yeshiva maintained traditions going back hundreds of years. One couldn't just wear the clothing without playing the part as well. Chayim's convictions in his faith were very strong. Whether Glenn agreed or not, this was the lifestyle that Howie had chosen, and like the friend he knew as a kid, once he put his mind to something, he committed himself with every inch of his being.

"But can you at least be a little straight-forward in suggesting something? Something like 'I'll be happy to do some work for you this summer since I'm not working and have a lot of time on my hands' kind of letter?"

"I don't have a lot of time on my hands Glenn," Chayim responded sternly as he defiantly crossed his arms in front of him.

"I know, I know. Just come up with an idea of why you're available."

"Fine. I'll think of something. We may be in for a wait, though. I can't imagine that replying to my email would be at the top of my Rosh Yeshiva's 'to do' list."

Glenn was feeling gutsy in his beer induced state. "Just be sure to send it out tonight," he pleaded, throwing the two empty beer bottles into the recycle bin that he had bought for his room. "You want another beer?"

"No thanks, I've got to study tonight. Another one, and I'll be shits for the night."

"You never cease to amaze me, toilet mouth," Glenn said while shaking his head in disbelief. "A holy guy who never cleaned up his foul mouth. Has the world ever seen such a disgrace?!"

Chayim got up from the bed. He had a shifty-looking grin on his face. "I'll get the email out tonight. *You* get me a copy of your new CD. I gotta go. Let's make some time this week to do something- it'll do us both good."

He walked out of Glenn's room, down the stairs and let himself out of the house. Glenn remained in his room, lying on his back, staring at the ceiling. All the stuff they had talked about really had his mind going.

11
May, 2012

Mohsen was a smart man, but he was also extremely impatient. The flight home seemed to last forever, even though it was a normal, smooth flight that he had taken so many times before. This time, the return trip from Vatican City was the longest of his life. Slowly, the minutes ticked by until they became the hours needed to make the trip home.

*   *   *

The phone rang. Awakened from a deep sleep, Afshin strained to look at the clock. It read one-eleven in the morning. For him, the only time the phone rang at this hour was so his boss could relay some bad news. This time was different.

"Hello?" Afshin responded as though he weren't sleeping. His boss hated people who weren't productive.

"I need you to look at something," was the reply from over the wire. "Can you meet me at the office lab in an hour?"

"Of course."

"Good. This is something that should arouse your passions. See you then."

Afshin hung up the phone. *Arouse his passions?* He wondered if his boss had found another good nugget in the archives. Nuggets; that was the term he and Mohsen referred to regarding the items of small value found in the Vatican's archives. But this one could not be any ordinary nugget, for Mohsen would not have called so early. He had never called in the middle of the night for one before.

Not a trace of guilt entered Afshin's mind when he thought about the information he was about to receive. Knowing full well these artifacts should have been turned over to the rest of the world decades, and in some circumstances, centuries ago instead of being kept as the exclusive prize for a very select few didn't bother him in the slightest. In fact, most of these privileged individuals were already dead. His boss just so happened to be one of the privileged individuals who wasn't dead.

Afshin's staunch, if not fanatical, views on the superiority of his religion led him to believe that any inhabitants outside of the world of Islam were merely created by God for the benefit of Muslims. His greatest passion, pushing for the Islamic goal of world domination, gave him the drive to become highly educated in Jewish and Christian texts, language, and culture. 'Know your enemy' was his mantra. He knew them well.

Eager to learn more of what his boss alluded to on the phone, Afshin quickly raced out of bed, threw on some clothes, hastily jumped into his car and drove to the office.

12
June, 2012
Denver, Colorado

Glenn was driving his mom's SUV into his parent's driveway when he saw Chayim, across the street, mowing the lawn of his mother's front yard.

"He looks ridiculous," Glenn smiled to himself, scrutinizing Chayim's grass-cutting attire. *"Eighty-five degrees outside and the goof is cutting grass in long sweatpants and a long sleeved tee-shirt. At least he's wearing a baseball hat instead of that black hat!"*

Chayim saw the SUV pulling up and observed Glenn getting out of the driver's seat with a big smirk on his face. He knew right then what the subject of Glenn's amusement was. He turned off the lawnmower and walked across the street, thinking of a good comeback for the wisecrack he knew was coming.

Glenn had sharp wit, but Chayim's yeshiva training had sharpened his thinking skills as well.

Glenn could hardly help himself, "I know you're dressing to be modest, Chayim, but can't you show at least a *little* bit of those stick legs you're hiding under there?"

Chayim was ready. Looking at his friend's over-sized tank-top which revealed a not-too-muscular and skinny upper torso, he replied, "The sages say, 'Sick minds are contained in sick bodies.' Need I say more?"

"Bastard," Glenn winced back.

The two met in the middle of the street and gave each other a brotherly hug.

"Where you coming from?" Chayim asked.

"My mom had me pick up some stuff from the grocery store. She's got Book Club tonight. A bunch of women choose a book to read and then get together once a month to discuss it, drink wine, and eat sushi. My mom's the sushi chef for the club, and I told her I'd get the ingredients and help her make it."

"Such a nice boy," Chayim teased with clenched teeth, pinching Glenn's left cheek.

Glenn cast aside his friend's arm, laughing. "Truthfully," he said, "I wanted to go. I know I'm going to get a couple of Spicy Tuna Rolls out of it. Plus, this is the only time I can get time to myself. Without my own transportation, I'm stuck. Hey, did you find anything out from your principal on that deal?"

Chayim shook his head. "No. I didn't expect my Rosh Yeshiva to volunteer anything of substance. But I do have some news. After I left your house I recalled hearing a lecture by a very famous rabbi on the topic of Good and Evil. In it, he mentioned the Staff. I hadn't heard the lecture in a while so I did a little digging and sure enough, I found the lecture on the net, and I was able to download it. In fact, I was going to come over with it as soon as I was done cutting the lawn. *Very* interesting stuff! Come over when you get a chance and we can listen to it together. Wait until you hear what's in this lecture- it's *really* fascinating."

"Let me get the groceries into the house and I'll be right there. I've been thinking about this thing the whole week! You really got my mind on fire!"

"I always told you that you'd be more religious than I."

"You're crazy," Glenn said as they departed to their respective houses.

*   *   *

Chayim's mom wasn't at home when Glenn rang the doorbell. Chayim opened the door and both he and Glenn went straight upstairs to Chayim's room. The room was a mess, as it always had been.

Glenn pushed some dirty clothes from the desk chair to find a place to sit down. His face displayed a look of disgust while he did so. "Some things just don't change," said Glenn.

"Nope," was the reply as Chayim moved the mouse around on his computer to locate the recording of the lecture.

Glenn looked at several piles of books stacked on the desk while Chayim messed around at his computer, getting frustrated that he couldn't find where he saved the lecture. Glenn took the top book from one of the piles and opened it. The pages were filled with a script that kind of resembled Hebrew, but unfamiliar to him. Glenn was impressed that Chayim could actually *read* the book, let alone understand it. Since his first trip to Israel, Glenn had wanted to be fluent in Hebrew, but never made the commitment to learn it.

Chayim finally found the downloaded lecture on his computer. He turned up the volume of the speakers. "Okay, so the recording quality pretty much sucks so you'll have to listen carefully. Plus, this rabbi's got a South African accent, which makes it even harder to understand."

With a click of the mouse, the lecture began. The rabbi was lecturing to a group of students. The subject matter, he explained, was about 'Evil' and he went on to expand on the 'hows' and 'whys' such a force could exist if God, the Ultimate Good, is truly Omnipresent. If that was the case, he stated, there could be no 'room' for Evil to even exist. Answering the 'why' part of the question was the easy one to answer; Evil is *necessary* for man to have free will. Without Evil, mankind would not be able to choose between good and bad, right from wrong. The question on *how* Evil could exist when God is the all-encompassing Good was the challenging part to answer.

Glenn listened to the lecture like the honor student he never was. Not once did he ask Chayim to stop the lecture and clarify a point, let alone argue it. He just sat on the desk chair leaning forward with his forearms on his knees, his hands folded. His head tilted a little to the left, as if leaning his right ear closer would facilitate better concentration.

The lecture continued.

"We read in Exodus, chapter three, about Moses being called by God from the burning bush, saying that he will be the messenger to free the Children of Israel from slavery. Moses then tries to plead his case that he is not the right man for the job. But God is persistent. In verse two of chapter four, God asks Moses 'What is that in your hand?' At first consideration, this sounds like a funny question. God knows everything. Why then does he have to ask Moses what is in his hand? *I'm* not God but even *I* would have had a pretty good idea of what was in Moses' hand!"

The audience chuckled.

"God is asking not for his own knowledge, but is really asking Moses, 'do you *really* know what it is you're holding? The Staff, says Kabbalah, was given to Moses due to its grave importance in world affairs. This Staff was present in the Garden of Eden. It was created from wood taken from the Tree of Knowledge. What does Genesis, chapter three, verse three say of the Tree of Knowledge? It says 'You shall neither eat of it nor *touch* it, lest you die.' What this is telling us is that the source of Evil in this world was constricted by God into The Tree of Knowledge, of Good and Evil. A section of the Tree was removed and the Staff was created. It was handed down, generation to generation from Adam, to Noah, to Abraham, Isaac, and Jacob, Joseph, and Moses. With all this in mind, let's go back to Exodus chapter four, verse three."

Glenn shook his head throughout the first part. He never learned about his religion this way. He began to understand why it never mattered to him like it did to Chayim. All Glenn could recall were the simple stories which mattered little in modern times. He became angry at his parents for not getting him a better education. The lecture continued.

"We see that God instructs Moses to put the Staff on the ground and it turns into a snake. The narrative then explains that 'Moses fled from it'. So here is Moses, in an intimate conversation with the Creator of the Universe, and yet he runs from a snake? The reason was the source of Evil in the Staff was so potent, even the greatest prophet, Moses, was afraid of it and needed to flee from its presence. God then taught Moses how to control the Evil, so that the Staff could be used to tap into the 'Good' potential it contained. This is why Moses was able to split the Red Sea with it, bring water from the rock, and so forth. But the fact remains, the Staff holds unbelievable power- beyond our wildest imaginations, for both the Good... *and* the Evil."

Chayim stopped the lecture at that point. The two of them sat silently for over a minute, completely awestruck.

Glenn spoke first, "And your principal told you guys about his dream about this very thing? And then the next day he's on the phone with secular professors of archeology in Israel? And you say that he generally doesn't have these fireside chats with secular professors?"

Chayim provided a continuous nod throughout the questioning.

"Jesus," said Glenn. "What in God's name, literally, is going on?"

"I don't know," replied Chayim. "But I have such a drive to find out."

Glenn sat on the chair, in thorough wonderment, shaking his head. "I can't believe I'm saying this, but feel like I do too," he said. "I know this sounds crazy, but I've gotta talk to your Rosh Yeshiva. Please Chayim, try and make the arrangements somehow."

"I know what you're thinking, Glenn, but there's no way he'll talk to you. If this is as deep as our imaginations are telling us, he's surely not going to talk to *us* about it. But...," Chayim's voice stopped in mid sentence.

"But, *what*?"

"But, I'm a step ahead of you. A buddy of mine is a student in a yeshiva in Jerusalem. He happens to be very familiar with the books of Genesis and Exodus. He's one-third archeologist, one-third historian, and one-third biblical scholar. I'm calling him tonight at ten our time. He emailed me yesterday and said he'd be available to chat at that time. I didn't tell him what it was about. Come over tonight, and we'll call him together."

"You got it," Glenn beamed as got up from the chair and exited the room. "I can't believe I'm liking this religion stuff. Now, if you'll excuse me, I have some sushi to make."

13
Tehran, Iran

His soul on fire, Afshin paced like a tiger while waiting for Mohsen to arrive; he always took the opportunity to arrive late. Doing so added an element of control. This time Afshin didn't mind. He was too busy anticipating what the item of interest might be. All the previous items that Mohsen involved him in paid off handsomely in both financial and religious terms. The privilege Mohsen enjoyed with private access to the Vatican archives bestowed him with documents of great historical importance. Were they to be exposed for the rest of the world to see, religion, government, and world power would drastically change. But for the select few with the means to acquire these treasures, personal gain was far greater a reward. Some of the artifacts were kept, while some were sold off to private European collectors for large sums of money. Though his share was modest, Afshin's cut still made him a wealthy man, but the money was secondary to him.

Afshin grew up during the Revolution of the late seventies. Iran had grown increasingly hateful of the West when the United States staunchly supported the Shah- a most hateful man from the revolutionary's perspective. Though most Iranians would tell stories of prosperity under the Shah's regime, according to the extremists, his rule was just another excuse to account for their own failures. Their hateful minds would never let go of their lack of power over the populace. A woman wearing jeans- considered clothing of the man and thus a sacrilege to Islam- would be brought to death if they could only have their way. Yet, secularity was commonplace among the streets of Tehran. And as a dedicated member among the young revolutionaries, Afshin promised himself that one day this would all change. Eventually, it did. The takeover of the United States Embassy during the Carter Administration was carefully orchestrated by the misguided rhetoric of the Muslim clerics, instilling the hatred needed to fuel the minds of the young and the gullible. They spewed words to anyone who would listen that democracy was despicable and warranted retribution for the secular values it imposed on their faith.

Afshin was not only an active participant in the takeover of the embassy, he was direct player in the planning of it. The Revolution needed and searched for a new charismatic leader inside the physical borders of Iran. The Ayatollah had been sent into exile and was living in France. The distance limited his ability to mobilize his young lions. It was during this time that Afshin's uncle was the needed charismatic figure with a big enough following that could bring the plan to fruition; an ultra-conservative cleric who used his pulpit as a means of denouncing the United States as 'The Great Satan'. The results were far greater than the old cleric could have possibly imagined, for not only did he influence the army to overthrow the Shah and takeover the Embassy, he also won the hearts of the young revolutionaries whose first order of business was to create a government after the takeover. As soon as the Ayatollah returned to Iran, the old cleric named Afshin's uncle as his number one commander.

After a lengthy wait, Mohsen's chauffeur-driven Mercedes pulled up next to the huge, two-story warehouse that served as his office and distribution plant. Mohsen climbed out the back of the limousine carrying the black briefcase that always accompanied him on his trips to the Archives. His four-person entourage filed in, two in front of him, two behind. They entered the secured building and took the private staircase up to the second floor suite. Afshin was there, awaiting them. As Mohsen entered, Afshin bowed to him. Mohsen walked a beeline to the humidity controlled room separated by clear glass adjacent to the main office space. He set the briefcase down on the large working table. He took off his suit coat, rolled up his sleeves and reached for two surgeon's gloves from a box on the side of the table.

"Aren't you at least going to give me a clue as to what you've found?" Afshin asked impatiently as Mohsen set up the workplace.

"I pay *you* to provide *me* with information, not the other way around," Mohsen snapped back coldly. "In time you will see, and be pleased."

Mohsen looked around the humidor to ensure the door was closed and that the humidifier was functioning properly. The gentle hum of the motor assured him it was. With everything in place, Mohsen unlocked the black briefcase and gently opened the top. Afshin was eager to see the contents and once the briefcase was open enough, inspected it closer. In the expandable strap sewn into the top which served to hold an ink pen was a clear, plastic tube with a length of roughly seven inches. Openings at both ends were sealed with rubber stoppers, similar to those used in laboratory test tubes to ensure the contents of the tube were held in place. Inside was the parchment.

"I was expecting something a bit, uh, bigger," Afshin mused scrutinizing the small tube.

Mohsen was unreactive. He held the tube like a fine gem, set it on the table, and proceeded to turn on the switch of the small, table humidifier. It was the same make the Vatican used for their vaults. He pulled on one of the end plugs of the tube and opened it. With tweezers, Mohsen carefully removed the parchment from the tube. He immediately held the paper in a direct line with the warm, moist air flowing out of the machine.

"I found this little piece of parchment stuck in the pages of a book written in Hebrew,' Mohsen announced.

"Do you know the date?" Afshin asked with a brash reflex. Mohsen knew the passion for religious history that his employee possessed.

"There is no apparent date, but I am guessing by the topics written in the book, that it comes from approximately the first or second century, A.D."

Afshin gathered Mohsen had taken the parchment without the permission of the Vatican. More than likely, they were the only ones in the entire world who were privy to the information written on the thin sheet. "I doubt even the Vatican librarians know of its existence. I certainly hope you've brushed up on your ancient Hebrew."

Afshin was irked by Mohsen's last sentence. Mohsen knew that Afshin was fluent in ancient and modern Hebrew. This, however, was Mohsen's discourteous way of emphasizing he expected the text to be translated with one hundred percent correct accuracy.

After several minutes of humidifying, the small parchment was ready to be opened without harm to it or the precious writing within it. Mohsen passed along a large, table-mounted magnifying glass which enabled Afshin to clearly see the contents of the parchment.

Afshin meticulously studied the wording, reading it over numerous times. Mohsen concealed his great anticipation and tried to relax because Afshin always took his time when he worked. Finally, Afshin spoke.

"The skin is in very good shape. It had to have been stored correctly right away."

"That is why I found it so enticing," Mohsen replied. "The book it was in contained notes written by a Hebrew scholar. It appears he was a marked man by the Romans and had to have been someone of notability."

Afshin drew his attention back to the parchment. As he peered through the glass, he instructed Mohsen to write down everything that he translated. Slowly, Afshin read:

"With the help of God, the One, the Creator. May He, in His mercy grant me pardon, as it is not by my wish that I write this information. Rather, by necessity, as I know that I am slated to be killed. Had my father not died before me, he too would have been sent to be crucified. Thus, since it is I alone who now has knowledge of the whereabouts of The Holy Staff of our teacher, Moses, in my memory, they will surely come for me. Since I cannot get to another and instruct him on its location before I am discovered, I must write the location down, praying for its guardianship, and this note become known only by the Holy, for the Staff is Holy and powerful."

Afshin momentarily looked blankly toward Mohsen then back. He turned the skin over and continued translating.

"I dreamed a holy dream where my brother, Levi, visited me in my sleep. He told me that he managed to remove the Staff from our father before the Romans seized it. Both he and the Staff sought refuge in the

Wilderness of the Negev. There in a cave, on the side of the tallest hill that the Creator has named 'The Mountain of the Dove'- that is the new resting place of The Holy Staff. That is all he told me. I pleaded with him to stay with me, but then I was awakened and I fear the dream confirms that he too is dead. 'The Mountain of the Dove.' May the Holy One guard the Staff and send his messiah quickly!"

Mohsen slowly fell back into a chair that was next to the table. He composed himself as he considered the enormity of information that was just translated to him. Afshin too, took on a look of wild-eyed astonishment.

"If this parchment is not part of some crazy ancient hoax," he stirred in excitement, "then it seems to me that we need to contact our allies in England. Tell them they need to book a trip to Palestine immediately, leaving by morning."

14

Glenn worked on his album before meeting with Chayim at his mom's house. An idea had finally popped into his head and he wanted to work it out while it was flowing. It was his first breakthrough since coming back to Denver and the new song was really coming together. He felt no pressure to make it work.

He paused momentarily to ponder whether the stories of the Staff were true, and whether they had any bearing on this sudden burst of creativity. Regardless, the music magically transposed from his mind to the electric piano and finally onto paper.

It felt good to finally have some positive energy infused into his work. In no time, the song was complete. Glenn went over it again on the piano, getting the last few kinks worked out. He played the piece one last time, perfectly. He gently pushed away from the keyboard and threw a clenched fist into the air in a gesture of victory.

The time on the clock by his bed read eight forty-seven. Enough time to get a beer, read the news off the internet, and head over to Chayim's for the conference call with the friend in Israel.

He went downstairs and heard his mom rushing to answer the ringing phone. A few seconds into the call, she yelled out for him to pick up the phone. It was Chayim.

"Hello?" Glenn said as he picked up the phone in the kitchen, opening the refrigerator door.

"Yo. Come over now- my buddy's on the other phone right now," Chayim responded quickly.

"I thought you guys said ten o'clock?"

"We did, but something came up. He called me early. He just got out of study. He can only talk for 15 more minutes so get over here."

Glenn closed the refrigerator. The call ended without so much as a 'good-bye'.

Glenn yelled out to his mom that he was going over to Chayim's house, to which she replied, 'OK, just be back by midnight.'

"Goo goo, dah dah," was the reply.

*   *   *

Upon entering the bedroom, Glenn saw Chayim sitting at his desk, writing down something on a piece of paper, while cradling the phone between his right ear and shoulder. Glenn didn't know why, but this was the first time he noticed Chayim was left-handed.

Without so much as looking up, Chayim waved Glenn to sit on the bed, nearby the phone sitting on the desk. At the same time, Chayim told his friend on the line that he was going to put him on the speakerphone so Glenn could hear as well. He pushed a button on the phone.

"You still there, Avner?" Chayim asked, unsure whether he had succeeded putting him on speakerphone or hung up on his friend.

"Still here," Avner confirmed. Glenn was amazed at the clarity of the connection. The last time he dialed internationally was ten years prior when his old girlfriend spent a year abroad, and the sound quality was less than great. Back then there was also a lot of delay, so the participants on the call would be continuously stepping on each other. But this call made it sound like Chayim's friend was across the street.

Chayim continued. "Glenn meet Avner, Avner meet Glenn."

Both parties blurted out salutations simultaneously. The result was a clash of mutual greetings, neither of which was understood by the other.

"Avner," Chayim continued, "we want you to tell us about the Staff of Moses. Specifically, if you know whatever became of it? I know the last we hear of Moses is at the end of Deuteronomy. After giving the Children of Israel a blessing and some instructions, he climbed Mount Nebo to die. But did he take the Staff with him?"

Silence was the reply on the other end of the line. After a long moment of this and fearing they had lost the connection, Chayim spoke again. "Hello? Avner?"

Avner answered in a passive monotone. "Yeah, I'm here."

"You okay?"

"Yeah." Another long pause, but not as long as the first time. "Sorry, I just wanted to make sure that I heard you correctly. Did you say you wanted to know about the Staff of Moses?" The question was rhetorical.

"Si," Chayim responded in Spanish to lighten the air of tension he sensed.

"Why do you want to know about the Staff?" Avner questioned tersely.

"Please don't say a word to anyone Avner, and it's probably nothing. But my Rosh Yeshivah told us about a dream he had regarding the Staff, and the next thing I know, he's on the phone with the head of the archeology department from Hebrew University. You know my Rosh Yeshiva- he didn't exactly see eye-to-eye with the secular professors. For him to call H.U. is *very* weird. We're just trying to figure out what's happening."

Silence ensued from the other end. Chayim put the phone on mute and he turned to Glenn shaking his head. "This doesn't sound like the Avner *I* know. Either he's multi-tasking while talking to us, or he's spacing..."

Avner interrupted and blurted out, "Chayim. I just got out of a study session with *my* Rosh Yeshiva. He just told us about a curious dream he had the night before- he dreamt about the Staff of Moses."

15
Somewhere Over the Atlantic Ocean

"I still can't believe we're doing this!" Glenn enthusiastically whispered from seat 23-A of El Al flight 1273 bound for Tel Aviv. Chayim occupied seat 23-B, trying to nod off.

"If you say that one more time, I'm going to ask you to be moved," Chayim responded with eyes half closed. "I knew you'd make googly eyes with the young stewardess, but I've got the older one on my side. She loves us nice, yeshiva boys. She told me we remind her of her kid. And all I have to do is tell her that you're affecting my ability to rest, and she'll be on you like flies to stink. So do us both a favor and shut up."

Glenn didn't respond, acting like he was fast asleep. Chayim prodded back, "I still can't believe we're doing this."

Glenn, eyes still shut, tried to suppress the smile on his face. When he failed to do so, he opened his eyes and grinned ear to ear.

"Whaddya think it all means?" Glenn said when seriousness returned. He saw Chayim wasn't trying to sleep anymore.

"I don't know, but when *two* Rosh Yeshivas have the same dream, something spiritual is trying to relay a message. Who knows how many more are out there that have had the same dream and not said anything about it."

"So you're saying this isn't coincidental?"

"No doubt in my mind."

The conversation compelled Glenn to ask more questions. "So what's the plan when we get there? Just get in a car and start looking for a big stick?"

"Avner told us to call him after we landed and got through passport check. He said there's a bus straight into Jerusalem. We should take it and then he'll pick us up from the Central Bus Terminal in the center of town. His yeshiva has a small car he can use to pick us up. From there, we'll go to the yeshiva and develop a plan of what to do."

"I've got the adrenaline pumping," Glenn replied ecstatically. "This plane isn't going fast enough!"

"Well you'd better figure out how to deal," said Chayim, "because you still have another six hours to go."

"Actually, there *is* something that I want to read," Glenn said. Let me see your books." Glenn reached for Chayim's backpack, under the seat in front of Chayim. He unexpectedly pulled out the Old Testament and handed it to Chayim. "Show me the section that talks about Moses talking to God at The Burning Bush. The part that says Moses ran from the Staff when it became a serpent. I want to read the whole thing this time. That stuff gave me shivers when you first told me about it and I want to see what happens now that I've learned a little more."

Chayim flipped through several pages to the beginning of Exodus. "Start reading here," he pointed. "It'll give you the whole story."

Glenn started reading. Studying the Bible unfortunately produced a predictable effect as Glenn was asleep in twenty minutes.

*   *   *

When he awoke, Glenn looked around. Chayim was fast asleep, as were most of the other passengers. He looked out the window. Wherever they were, it was nighttime, so all was black, with the exception of a few reading lights scattered inside the cabin. He checked his watch, now set for Tel Aviv time. Three more hours to go.

Glenn picked up reading where he had left off. He felt, deep inside, something unusual was going on. He didn't want to use the term 'spiritual' like Chayim did, but he did admit that 'coincidental' didn't cut it either. When shivers surged down his spine a second time as he read the passage of the Staff transforming into a serpent, he just couldn't shake the idea from his head that something truly monumental was at hand. He felt an inexplicable connection that made him want to break into the cockpit and accelerate the flight.

He remembered what that Rabbi on the internet lecture said about the Staff- *the original source of Evil in this world...*

16
Israel

As restless as he was on the plane, Glenn now was exhausted from the ten hour flight from New York to Tel Aviv. The trip, though, provided him time to further contemplate what he was reading. Plus, the more he learned from the Old Testament, the greater his curiosity, excitement and uncertainty grew. A week ago the Old Testament was two steps above make believe; an insignificant part of his life. Now that he was part of Chayim's inner circle, the stories he read, if authentic, were amazing beyond belief. This all made him rethink Chayim's world of spirituality and metaphysics really might be legitimate, and that God really did create the entire Universe. If this were indeed the case, then God really was The Ultimate and logically, there really is another realm above the physical world. If that were true, then the other realm would be more awesome than the physical universe.

The exhaustion and the enlightenment set Glenn's mind on fire.

The plane landed at four fifty-seven a.m. at Lod International Airport, just outside Tel Aviv. After their passports were verified and their luggage arrived, Chayim called Avner and they found their way to the bus depot of the airport. Both friends were amazed at how much bus service was happening, even at five in the morning. They found the bus to Jerusalem and boarded. Five minutes later, the vehicle departed.

*   *   *

The bus rolled into the main terminal just outside of downtown Jerusalem, roughly an hour later. Once inside the terminal, Chayim looked out the glass window, smiling and signaling to two bearded men standing outside by an old car on the curb. Glenn followed Chayim as he exited the bus. Chayim walked quickly up to Avner and they hugged and patted each other on the back, while the second person walked up to Glenn and introduced himself.

"Hi, I'm Yossi," he said, shaking Glenn's hand. Chayim then introduced his friend to Avner.

"A pleasure to finally meet you, Avner," Glenn said with sincerity.

Avner returned the greeting. "To you as well, Glenn. I love your music, by the way."

Glenn's exhausted-looking face lit up. "You've heard my music?"

"Sure have. The whole yeshiva has heard some songs from the MP3s Chayim sent me a couple of months ago. Your songs really show how much spirit is inside. You can understand that means a lot to a group of Bible fanatics."

Glenn looked at Chayim who was all smiles. Chayim winked back.

"Pirating my music I see."

"Consider me your marketing director to the religious world."

Avner opened up the trunk for the luggage. The trunk hinges to the old European auto squealed in resistance of having to be moved from its original rusty position.

The four got into the car, Avner driving with Yossi in the front passenger seat; Glenn and Chayim seated in the back.

"How was your flight?" Avner asked, starting the car. Glenn mused at the sudden thought that everybody always asks that same question. The car pulled noisily away from the curb.

"Not too bad," Glenn replied. Chayim looked at him, questioning the sincerity of the reply. He knew better.

Daybreak was beginning to lighten the eastern sky. The city was starting to wake as a few cars and people filtered into the streets. Glenn admired the passing display of Jerusalem from the back seat of the car, trying to take in all he could of the city. Not far off he could hear the beautiful chanting of the Muslim 'Call to Prayer' over a P.A. system. The whole Jerusalem ambiance was magical.

He watched as they passed through central downtown Jerusalem into a neighborhood to the north which resembled seventeenth century Poland. Men walked down the old tattered streets wearing long black coats that went past their knees and each wore different types of black hats. It was as if one could be affiliated with a particular community based on the hat one wore. Their sideburns were curly and hung down far past their ears. All but the young had beards. Glenn speculated that they were on their way to morning prayers. He also noticed that the houses of the neighborhood were elaborate shacks, easily a hundred-plus years old, and had probably never been upgraded since. The old stones of the buildings told amazing stories that cried out to Glenn who only imagined what a tour guide might say about them. This place was indeed spiritual, and it made a deep impression on Glenn. He really wanted someone to tell him all about this place and its history, and he hoped this trip would present the opportunity.

Tiny shops on the ground level of the two-story buildings were no more than a hundred square feet each. There was little evidence of technology, with the exception of a street lamp every hundred feet or so. These people were the ultra-religious, completely opposite from western society.

Chayim and Avner continued their small-talk, avoiding the subject which brought Chayim and Glenn eight-thousand miles east. Yossi, meanwhile, never moved, keeping his gaze fixed straight ahead. He looked like a mannequin.

Glenn didn't show it or say anything, but suddenly he became uncomfortable. He was in a new country, driving through a foreign neighborhood, with little money, and feeling like he was getting into something way over his head. He began to second-guess himself. He tried to ease the fire that started to well up in his gut and hoped that jumping back into the conversation would calm him down. "What's this place called?" he asked to anyone listening.

"We're passing through a small neighborhood in north Jerusalem. It's called Meah Sh'Arim," Yossi replied without so much as turning one muscle in his neck to look back at Glenn. It now seemed to Glenn that for Yossi, driving in a car, or at least a car with Avner driving, was not a pleasurable experience.

The car passed a few blocks beyond Meah Sh'Arim and came to a stop in front of an old building, which appeared the same as every other one they had seen. The condition of the car matched the condition of the building. The four got out of the car and entered the building. No one spoke. Glenn felt some apprehension and if Chayim did too, he certainly didn't show it. Yossi bore off to the left, down a hall and entered a small office whose walls were obscured with bookshelves, all brimming with books. Even the desk had several piles of loosely stacked books, plus two more already opened appearing to be someone's unfinished learning. Avner brought up the rear of the group, carrying additional chairs to accommodate everyone in the small office. They all took a seat, leaving the main chair of the desk unoccupied, as it was obviously reserved for the Rosh Yeshiva.

Almost instantly a small man with a long white beard that grew down past his neckline walking with the assistance of a cane slowly made his way into the room. Chayim, Yossi, and Avner simultaneously stood up as the little old man walked straight towards the new arrivers. Glenn looked at the others and figured that he should stand as well. The man hugged Chayim. Seeing this, Glenn assumed the two were close, or possibly related. But when Chayim introduced himself after the embrace, Glenn realized this man had a love for his brother without even knowing his name. The old man displayed true modesty for someone who commanded such respect. After receiving Chayim's introduction, the man introduced himself as Rabbi Lindow and with that, he turned his attention to Glenn, who also received a hug.

"Hi, my name is Glenn," Glenn said awkwardly.

"Gentlemen," said the Rabbi, "it is my honor that you traveled all the way to Israel for my benefit. I am truly grateful. Please, everyone, sit down so that we may discuss matters."

Glenn still felt tense. *"What are we involved in, that this man, who seems to have better things to do than chit-chat with us, is actually chit-chatting with us?"* he thought to himself.

Avner got right to the point. "Chayim, what do you think the chances are that one, both our Rosh Yeshivas dreamt similar dreams about the Staff of

Moses around the same time, two, that they were bothered enough to tell their students about it, and three, that you picked up the phone to call me and ask me about the Staff?"

"Well, the rational person in me wants this to be a mere coincidence, but when you told me about Rabbi Lindow's dream, the word coincidence just doesn't fit."

"True. That's why Rabbi Lindow had me call you to come out here, as all of these pieces together warranted a face-to-face meeting."

"But I'm confused Rabbi," Glenn broke in. "Chayim didn't have the dream, his *Rosh Yeshiva* did. And though he told the students about it, they're not even supposed to know the details. Why wouldn't you just call him directly?"

"I did," replied the rabbi. "But when I spoke to him about it, he became very upset with me. Chayim, I mean no disrespect to your rabbi, but he's old school, and wanted to consult with his superiors before doing anything about it. In fact, he very much regretted that he told his students about it in the first place. I'm afraid if something is happening, that he and his superiors will delay for too long. I'm a maverick and I want to know now. Maybe this is all a crazy set of circumstances and not related at all. But I'd rather know that sooner than later. So, I asked Avner to get on the phone and invite you over to have this little chat."

Glenn looked at the rabbi. He found it amusing that this unassuming old man called someone else 'old school'.

Chayim remained silent, analyzing all of the information in his head. Glenn seized the opportunity to continue to throw in his two cents. "Rabbi, I'm not a very religious guy. And I don't really believe in fate and am probably the most skeptical one in this room. But I can just *feel* something is happening, based on everything I've learned from Chayim over the last several days! Speaking on behalf of my friend here, I think he *wants* to tell you about his Rabbi's dream, but is afraid of a breach of trust. So, if you will allow whatever your plan is to include *me* too, then *I* will tell you. Chayim can then remain in good conscience and he won't get in any trouble. For my part, I really don't care if I get in trouble. So, if you tell me what you're thinking, *I* will try to provide the other details."

Rabbi Lindow, staring at Glenn, paused several moments before replying.

"Okay, listen carefully," he said as he leaned forward onto the desk. "I had an extremely vivid dream about two weeks ago. In the dream I was in a mountainous desert. I don't know why I was there, except that I was looking up from the base of a small, rocky hill. At the top of the hill was a large boulder that would have appeared more natural at the basin rather than the top, where it stood. At least that way, it would be evident the rock was once a part of the mountain and had eventually broken off and fallen. But this rock was curiously positioned at the top of the mountain. So from where could it have broken off? I started climbing the mountain to get a better view of the rock and as I did so, I saw a white dove that had

been circling in the sky come down and rest on top of
the very same rock. As soon as the bird landed on top
of the rock, the rock shifted to the left, exposing the
opening to a cave. Out of the cave came a young man,
about your age and he was holding a staff in his hand."

The same wonderful and awe-inspiring feeling
that Glenn had felt the night when Chayim recited the
Old Testament story of Moses' Staff had begun to stir
within him again. He knew where the old sage's story
was going, but he wanted to hear it anyway. Glenn
changed his position on his chair and leaned closer to
the rabbi. He found it difficult to sit still.

The rabbi continued relaying his dream. "At first
I thought I was having a vision of Moses and his Staff.
After all, other than Charlton Heston, who really knows
what Moses looked like?" The old man chuckled at his
own humor and the rest of the group chuckled with
him.

"But for some unknown reason I knew this man
was not Moses- just a man. He looked at me and, as he
saw that I was watching, hugged the Staff as a father
hugs his child. The staff was obviously special to the
man. And then... I could see why. In the sunlight, the
Staff reflected brilliantly the most dazzling piece of blue
sapphire I have ever seen hewn into the shaft. I started
to cry because I knew immediately whose Staff this
was. But why did this man, whom I did not recognize,
have the Staff? Before I could come up with an answer,
a large hawk swooped down and grabbed the Staff from
the man. He made no attempt to struggle with the
hawk, as if he was not allowed to resist. But then, the

white dove darted in and fought with the hawk. I watched helplessly as this little white dove fought fiercely with the giant hawk. Each had a firm grasp on the Staff as they clawed and pecked and snapped at one another. I was truly frightened, as I waited to see who would be the victor. Unfortunately, I snapped awake and struggled desperately to close my eyes and fall asleep again so I could see the outcome. But to no avail. The adrenaline was already pumping through my body, and I could not manage to fall back asleep again. I have gone over the dream in my mind time and again. I poured through all of the references to the scriptural verses that mention Moses' Staff and after all that I've read, I'm *convinced* that someone has stumbled onto the whereabouts of the Staff... and that something of epic proportions is going to happen. It could be either magnificent or terribly destructive which is why, I believe, I was not allowed to see which bird would win."

Chayim looked at Glenn who was trying not to show it, but his eyes were welling up with tears. All this, combined with the exhaustion of traveling for the last twenty-four hours had climaxed. He knew too that two dreams dreamt by two such wise sages was no coincidence.

He thought of all the elements that were bringing this whole picture together; his inability to write music in New York, his decision to come home for a while, Chayim being on break from his yeshiva and coming into town at the same time, the night they had the beers, talking about Old Testament stories, the dream by Chayim's rabbi, and now the dream of this rabbi. It was all too much. Glenn believed in God, but it was never something he acted on and now he felt guilty from not even attending synagogue in over seven years. He cried, silently, using his shirtsleeve to wipe his nose.

The rabbi handed Glenn a tissue from his top desk drawer. "I'm sorry," said Glenn as he took the tissue.

"Don't be sorry," Rabbi Lindow replied. "What do you think was the first thing I did when I woke up from my dream?" Rabbi Lindow's superbly gentle manner made Glenn feel so comfortable with the man, that he felt an instant bond.

Chayim chimed in as Glenn gathered himself. "Rabbi," he said, "I would like to tell you about my Rabbi's dream. What you have revealed goes far beyond any trouble I might get into with my Rabbi. I am a student of biblical texts and I do not believe in mere coincidence. Something truly awesome is brewing, and we are sitting at your desk in the middle of Jerusalem for a reason."

Rabbi Lindow smiled. Even still, a look of concern draped across his face. "Do what you feel is right in your heart," he said.

"I know what's right," Chayim said with conviction. "But first, can you elaborate on what became of the Staff after Moses died?"

"I can't, but I know of someone who can. Are you alert enough from your travels to meet him?"

Glenn spoke first. "I don't know about Chayim, but I'd stay up another twenty-four hours to hear this!"

Rabbi Lindow slowly rose from his chair. "Let's take a little walk," he said.

17

The foursome followed the hobbling old man out the main door of the yeshiva. The rabbi's gait was limiting, but no one seemed to mind. Glenn thought the slow pace would actually give him a chance to play 'tourist'. He watched the inhabitants of this community on their daily routines.

But the tourist mode quickly switched from excitement to a feeling of foreboding anxiousness. From the exhaustion, excitement and uncertainty, his anxieties started to culminate on his mental peace of mind. He also felt the culture shock. To him, walking down these old streets was like walking into a time capsule. One day before he was in the modern suburbs of a twenty-first century American city and then just like that, he was in one of old Jerusalem's oldest and poorest neighborhoods containing people who looked like they belonged in seventeenth century Poland. He was not in control and fought off that panic. He had to concentrate to try and roll with the feelings so they didn't get the best of him. In all the times performing his music in front of thousands of people he never experienced anxiety as greatly as he was experiencing it now. To reduce the stimulation he stopped looking about and just focused on the sidewalk ahead of him. That calmed him a bit since the sidewalks there resembled those of New York City.

In their short walk from the yeshiva front door, the group had walked one block when the street broke off into a series of alleyways that littered both sides of the street. Rabbi Lindow passed two alleyways but took a right turn to enter the third. As dilapidated as the main street was, this alleyway was worse. The cracking of the housing structures was rampant and the old steel catwalks that served as the structure's afterthought to escaping fire were loosely attached to the buildings they served. Swaths of missing mortar on the structure's faces disclosed their age. Many of the windows no longer contained glass- rather they had either been replaced by wood inserts or wall-unit air conditioners. Stray cats were in abundance, searching for what little daily nutrition was contained in the dozens of trash cans that either stood or were lying toppled on their sides.

The end of the alleyway was fifteen yards ahead and contained one solitary concrete staircase which led down to a basement area three yards below. Rabbi Lindow put his cane in his left hand while he held onto the rusting metal banister that was starting to pull from the side concrete wall. Yossi hurried to get in

front of the rabbi since he wanted to avoid the avoidable
which would have sent the little old sage tumbling
down the stairs. Once at the bottom, the rabbi knocked
on the door with the handle of his cane.

Roughly one minute later another old man, even
shorter than Rabbi Lindow, opened the door. He looked
at the group without so much as an expression of
emotion. His face told many stories, but they weren't
happy ones. Rather, it displayed stories of sadness and
despair. He did not smile when he saw Rabbi Lindow.
Instead, he broke off into a whispered Yiddish
discussion with Rabbi Lindow and the four young ones
waited uncomfortably for it to end. After time, the old
man reluctantly shrugged his shoulders and Rabbi
Lindow motioned for all of them to enter the basement
room.

The group entered into a small room roughly
three yards square. The walls were lined with
bookshelves and upon them were stacks and stacks of
books haphazardly resting on them. In the back of the
room was a little kitchenette that contained a sink, a
small refrigerator and a towel rack that held two dirty
white towels. A door to the left of the kitchenette
opened into a small bathroom. A cot was leaning
against the left wall, a clear indication that it was the
source of where the old man slept and was placed out of
the way when not in use. One chair was available and
the old man motioned for Rabbi Lindow to sit down.
Yossi, Avner, Chayim and Glenn stood on both sides of
the sages.

The man attempted no communication with the lads. Glenn suspected that no English was spoken here.

"Boys, this is Reb Wein," Rabbi Lindow said. Reb Wein nodded his head to the boys when he heard his name.

"Reb Wein is righteous man. He is a Kabbalist and one of the 'thirty-six'.

"Thirty-six?" asked Glenn respectfully.

"The existence of the world rests for the sole reason that thirty-six hidden righteous people keep it from being destroyed. Their role in life is to justify the purpose of mankind in the eyes of God; their identity is unknown to themselves, each other and to the rest of the world."

"Sorry, but another question," Glenn responded, "If he's supposed to be secret, then how come he revealed himself to us?"

"He didn't reveal himself to you," Rabbi Lindow answered. "I did. This man doesn't understand a word I'm saying to you, and he doesn't even know he's one of the thirty-six. I've lived in this community long enough to know that he is. This man has done more for the world than the world could even begin to know. The stories I could tell you about what this man has endured. He's witnessed a lot."

The man just looked at the group without expression. Rabbi Lindow turned to Reb Wein and began speaking to him.

Trying to listen and pick out a few words, Glenn realized they weren't speaking Hebrew. "Is that Yiddish?" he whispered to Chayim.

"Yes," Chayim whispered back. "The people of this inner core of observance only use Hebrew when studying texts or praying. It's too holy of a language to use in everyday speech."

"Isn't that a little extreme?"

"Some may think so. But these people know that most of the things people talk about are so trivial that it's not fitting to use God's language for idle chit-chat. So they use Yiddish instead for the everyday talk."

Glenn nodded his head as he thought about what Chayim just said.

After talking for a long time, Reb Meir stopped talking so Rabbi Lindow could translate to the boys what he said.

"This much he knows about what happened to the Staff," the rabbi started to answer. "Moses was about to die and gave his charge to Joshua. Tradition tells us that Moses handed the Staff to Joshua at that point, since he was trained by Moses personally to learn how to control its power. Reb Meir has even found sources, none of them widely accepted, that the walls of Jericho were toppled not by the sounds of the trumpets, but by Joshua's use of the Staff. Even though the book of Joshua doesn't say anything about him using the Staff, several oral accounts of the usage are recorded. But when Joshua is about to die no commentary says anything about him transferring the Staff to the next leadership. But Reb Meir says that Joshua transferred the Staff to the High Priest who transferred it down to the subsequent Priest, and on and on from generation to generation."

When Rabbi Lindow stopped talking, Reb Meir resumed. Even though the four young men couldn't understand much, they were entranced by the little man and hung onto every word. Chayim teared up a bit as he looked at Reb Meir, thinking about all this poor man has endured, yet still holds onto the highest of observance.

"King Solomon built the first Temple," Rabbi Lindow continued. "But while a massive number of workers built what was above the ground, an equal number of workers were busy beneath the Temple's mount digging out an incredible maze of catacombs. It was built deliberately complex because King Solomon had been shown the prophecy that one day his magnificent Temple would be destroyed when the Jews faltered in their observance to God. Thus, he knew in advance that the very awesome and holy structure he was building would eventually be destroyed. But he had to continue to build anyway, in hopes that that prophecy would not come to pass. Sadly it did, but the High Priest of that time wisely took precautions and hid the Ark of the Covenant, the Staff and other items from the Temple in the catacombs."

Glenn kept asking more questions. He had the most catching up to do. "The Ark of the Covenant? Like in the movie?"

Everyone nodded.

"Isn't that more valuable than the Staff? Why were the dreams about the Staff when the Ark is more valuable?"

Rabbi Lindow answered the question. "The Ark is more valuable in terms of what it contains and what it is made of. It's pure gold and contains the original Five Book of Moses. But its religious, historical and monetary values are nothing compared to the powers that emanate through the Staff."

Reb Meir spoke one last time and Rabbi Lindow solemnly translated.

"Directions of how to access the catacombs were passed from King Solomon himself to one family that he trusted. That family was given charge of keeping the knowledge of the catacombs a total secret and the directions were to be handed down orally to the next generation. Eventually the Temple was rebuilt but the items were kept hidden in case of another attack. Hundreds of years later, the Romans had somehow gotten wind of the knowledge that the Staff was still buried beneath the Temple mount and they managed to infiltrate the catacombs. They were slowly closing in on the Staff's location, thus prompting the descendants of the family to have the Staff retrieved before Pontius Pilate seized it."

Rabbi Lindow started to get choked up. The thought hit him like a ton of bricks. He pulled a handkerchief from his pockets and wiped his eyes.

"The Staff, Reb Meir says," he choked out, "was smuggled away from Jerusalem to a new location, and he speculates that it lies somewhere in the Negev Desert."

Rabbi Lindow couldn't control himself and broke into a full-fledged sobbing.

"My dream... The Mountain of the Dove. My dream was revealing to *me* the *new* hiding place of Moses' Staff!"

18

Back at the yeshiva the four young men had gathered into the library to start the search. Two hours later, Chayim looked up from the text he was reading and warily cast his eyes on Avner and Yossi who were wide awake and engrossed in their own research. It was now close to forty hours since they left home and the fatigue was taking its toll on his ability to concentrate.

His gaze passed over to Glenn who was sitting at a desk, slumped over one of the few books written in English and fast asleep. That was okay, Chayim mused to himself, since Glenn couldn't even read the foreign texts necessary for the research, let alone understand them. He got up and stretched, walked around the room to improve the circulation in his legs and dutifully sat back down to continue the search for any reference to the 'Mountain of the Dove'.

Several hours later, Chayim again looked up. He must have dozed off a bit. Now his back hurt. As he stretched from a hunched position he observed his friends in the room one more time. Glenn was in the same position as he had been hours earlier. Chayim smiled to himself. Poor Glenn, what a neck ache he was going to have when he woke up!

Suddenly Yossi screamed out in total excitement. "I found it! I found the reference!" Glenn was startled to consciousness.

He looked around at everyone and motioned for them to gather around the yellowed pages he was researching. Everyone quickly jumped out of their seat upon hearing the news. They all quickly gathered around Yossi. He had been hunched over a rather large, old book; its pages yellowed by time. It was an old copy of the Aleppo Codex.

"The 'Mountain of the Dove,'" said Yossi. "Right here in the Codex!"

"I've heard of the Codex," said Chayim, "but I really don't know what's in it."

Yossi answered him. "Most people don't, including scholars. Not many resources have been made public."

"But what's in it?"

Yossi was eager to answer that question. "It's mostly a manuscript of the Hebrew bible. Manuscripts were so rare at the time. So the religious value of the book was great, as it could be used for teaching the masses in a much simpler manner. The Codex was written in the tenth century and was given to the

Jewish community of Jerusalem during the mid-eleventh century. However, it was among the works held ransom by the Crusaders during the First Crusade. After being rescued by the elders of a town called Ashkelon, it was transported to Egypt along with Jewish refugees for safekeeping, and later resurfaced in Cairo, where it was consulted by Maimonides. His descendants eventually brought it to Aleppo, Syria at the end of the fourteenth century. The Codex remained there for five-hundred years, until Muslim anti-Jewish riots desecrated the synagogue where it resided. The Codex disappeared, and re-emerged in 1958, when it was smuggled into Israel. Once in Israel, it was found that the secret parts of the Codex had been lost, or removed."

Chayim was impressed at Yossi's knowledge. But he was also puzzled. "But if it is only a copy of the Old Testament, then shouldn't everyone know what's in it?"

"No," Yossi replied with soft confidence. "It's not only a copy of the Old Testament. The part of the Codex that was lost is known to have personal writings attached to it; writings by the sages of the Kabbalah. Copies of those writings can be found in only a select few yeshivas and are studied by even fewer."

"But if the writings of the lost part of the Codex exist," Chayim said, "then why aren't they brought to the original and added back in?"

"The secular world would only bastardize the find. They'd make a media circus out of it. Then they'd make a movie. Then, when the dust settled, they would

136 | Jeff Wedgle

throw it under glass in a museum and charge people eight dollars to come view it. That's as far as it would go; no care to think about it again. For the religious, these things are sacred; to be studied and cherished. They have the best of both worlds while the secular world just speculates and debates. Did it happen or didn't it? Was it written by man or God? Is it true or just stories? The list goes on and on, and so do they. The secular world goes into a 'circular reference', as computer programmers call it. Their interest in the metaphysical ebbs and flows with the state of the economy. When things are good, who needs God? When things are tough, they wonder where God is. The cycle only repeats itself. But the religious world will ultimately present it for all to see when the world is finally ready for it. Until then..." Yossi faded off. He finally girded his emotions regarding his distaste for this particular quality of the secular world.

Chayim asked Yossi, "So is this the first book of those that contain the lost part?"

"Yes. I had a hunch. Why would *our* rabbi have the dream and not other great sages around the world? Then I thought of things that made him unique. He's a great man, but so are the other sages. Then, in my exhaustion, I let my mind go and poof- the Codex popped in my mind! I knew that our rabbi was one of the few who have a hidden copy of the full Aleppo Codex. I have access to his locked library, so I went and got it. I went straight to the missing sections of the Codex, and scoured through them, and two hours later, there it was... 'The Mountain of the Dove'. If I wasn't so exhausted, I probably would have missed it!" Yossi smiled with satisfaction, clasping his hands behind his head as he leaned back into his chair.

"If what you're saying is true, then I'll bet *my* rabbi has a copy of the Codex!" exclaimed Chayim as he finally grasped the correlation.

"I would tend to agree with that," said Avner. "And I'll bet at least a dozen other great sages around the globe have it and had a similar dream. Either they don't know about others dreaming about the Staff, or are worried and waiting until something else develops."

Glenn couldn't control his enthusiasm. "Yossi, you're a genius!"

"Yossi studied at the Hebrew University before coming to our yeshiva," Avner explained. "He wasn't religious at all before his studies at the Hebrew U. That training gives him an edge."

"I majored in Biblical History there," answered Yossi. When I was there, my name was Joey. 'Joey, the fat kid from Baltimore'."

"You're kidding!" Glenn chirped from behind the three of them. "You look so authentic! You mean at one time you were actually like me? What made you become religious?"

"I loved history. And the more I read, the more I found secular history to be incomplete, relative and speculative. So, to fill in the gaps, I came to a yeshiva. I had no intention of becoming observant until one day those gaps *were* getting filled in. Then something inside of me realized that this stuff *has* to be true. So, I became religious out of conviction, not really desire."

Glenn could totally relate to that.

"I don't know about you all," chimed Avner, who had had enough of the lollygagging, "but I would really love to know what the Codex says about the Mountain of the Dove. Can we please proceed?"

Yossi turned to the old book that lay in front of him. He used a magnifying glass to look at a particular section. "Write down what I translate," he said openly, not waiting for anyone in particular. Avner knew where to find a pen and paper in the rabbi's office, which meant he accepted the task by default. Yossi proceeded with the text:

"...*Jerusalem, the Center of the physical Universe, is the foundation for the redemption of man. Firstly, Redemption shall descend from the Mountain of the Dove, which is in the mountains of Judea. But the white dove will be seen for one of two reasons; at the time of danger and the time of redemption. Mankind will not know which it is...*"

The room went silent again, but this time, it was not from exhaustion. All four of the young men knew what was required next; an extended tour of the Judean Hills, east of Jerusalem, of which the Rosh Yeshiva would gladly approve.

19
Judean Desert
East of Jerusalem

Glenn scanned the scenery as he drove the car east, toward the Dead Sea. As expected, Chayim, Yossi and Avner were fast asleep from their all-night research marathon. Glenn was exhausted as well. This time as he looked around, there was no anxiety; only the excitement of being in the Holy Land and as a result resorted to taking in all that he saw. The drive from Jerusalem on Highway One was magical. Though barren, the Judean Hills carried a spiritual quality that one could literally feel. All this talk of biblical stories had taken Glenn back in time as he easily reflected on his religious school days growing up.

He hated going there. Twice a week after regular school and Saturday mornings it was the same old thing; the dread of *more* school after an already long day at secular school. And, to make things worse, instead of Saturday morning being a day of cartoons and football, it was a day to dress up in a monkey suit and go listen to some ill-qualified adult telling them inaccurate or irrelevant stories or simply consuming the entire time futilely ordering the class to be quiet. Glenn's mom was a religious woman though not really an observant one. She never had the option to learn about Judaism. Growing up in a meager home in Cheyenne, her family never had the money to send her to Hebrew school, so she viewed Hebrew School as an opportunity, not a burden. As a result, Glenn's little league days were few and he resented his mom for this, since she and Glenn's father didn't even attend services while Glenn was in class. They would simply drop him off to go run errands.

Apparently Glenn had learned something in those days, however. The once uninspired stories he remembered- pretty much the basics such as Noah and the Ark, Adam and Eve and the Garden of Eden, and the Tower of Babel- came alive as he drove through the barren hills of the Judean Desert. He imagined them with great excitement, thinking they could easily have occurred right here where he was driving.

The road to the Dead Sea had markers posted at periodic intervals informing travelers they were heading below sea level. At one thousand three hundred eighty feet below sea level, they were en route to the lowest point on the face of the earth. This was thrilling for Glenn, though no one was awake to share his elation.

Highway One ended at the northern tip of the Dead Sea and forked into a north-south running road. The northern road was a shortcut up to the Sea of Galilee, passing by the Biblical town of Jericho. South headed toward the Dead Sea's west shore and Masada. Glenn made the right turn and took the road south. He immediately passed a sign marked 'Qumran' which he knew to be where the ancient Dead Sea Scrolls were found. He reveled in sheer exultation. Though they were on an important 'mission', Glenn couldn't keep the tourist in him at bay. As they advanced, the most beautiful scenery opened up before him; the Dead Sea's crystallized water to the left and the edge of the Judean Hills to the right. He was in awe. Everyone else was still out cold.

Glenn was reluctant to wake the others up. They had done the work the previous night with maybe an hour of rest, but he didn't know where he was going. He woke them as they arrived at the turnoff where Avner had previously told him to turn. The sign read 'Ein Gedi' as Glenn announced the location of their old, beat up car. The sleepy passengers stirred. Avner, the first to actually respond, instructed Glenn on the next set of directions.

"About a mile or so further you'll see a turnoff to the 'Ahava Skin Care' Company," he said half-consciously. Take that road up and you'll see the manufacturing plant on the right. Go past it and take the dirt road that winds off into the hills." He then tried to go back into a slumber.

The directions were perfect and Glenn noticed the dirt road just ahead. He turned the car onto the road and immediately noticed that the drive would have to be taken slowly. The dirt road was curvy and bumpy, meandering toward the heart of the Judean Desert. The landscape was hilly, barren and beautiful. Awakened by the rocking of the car along the ill-maintained path, all four passengers were now fully awake. They took in the sights, each connecting spiritually, sharing stories they had once learned about the area. As each told their own story, they all visualized the awesome display of the Divine.

"What is our plan?" Glenn asked changing the topic to address the current situation. "Just drive until we see a dove?"

Yossi responded. "We're going to drive into the center of the desert. There's a little area I know well, and I'm going on a hunch that it is the first place to begin looking for clues. Keep driving on this road for about another fifteen miles. At that point there's a hellacious dirt road that turns south. We're going to take that road about five miles to a wonderfully isolated spot that I've been to many times."

Chayim displayed a curious look on his face. "A road worse than this? What motivates a man to want to visit some place 'many times' when risking life and limb to get there?"

"Look, I wasn't *always* a religious guy," Yossi replied. "I mean, I guess I've always been religious, but not terribly observant. My first few trips to Israel were for hiking and camping out. We originally came across this place while searching for a location to plant a little 'garden'."

Chayim became even more curious. Thinking about what Yossi said about a garden make him think of the only thing that made any sense. And when it dawned on him what kind of garden they were cultivating, he did a double-take at Yossi who was staring straight ahead, as usual, except this time he donned a grin from ear to ear. Never in a million years would Chayim have guessed that in his formal life, Yossi was a stoner. Even more, he risked expulsion from the country with a mark on his record that he never be allowed to return to Israel. All this just to grow hash.

"It was either grow it ourselves, or buy it from the Arabs," Yossi confessed. "Times then were too tumultuous for us to go into the Arab villages and buy it. So, we decided to take our hobby out to nature. No one would ever suspect a bunch of stupid American tree-eaters to do anything like what we were doing. It was the perfect storm. We really had a good thing going for a couple of years."

Now it was Glenn's turn to get in on the conversation. He too simply couldn't believe that the pious Jew in the front seat, well versed in his studies, was actually a dope smoking goof that was crazy enough to cultivate his own plantation in the middle of no man's land. The situation took on a whole new light, as Glenn now felt less alienated and intimidated by his fellow hunters. The new information leveled the playing field and he finally felt completely comfortable with these guys. Out of all the questions Glenn wanted to ask Yossi, "Where'd you get the water?" was all he could muster.

"There were some local Bedouins that maintained a well nearby. We exchanged a portion of our crop for some of their water. We were out one night in downtown Jerusalem, getting high with some friends we met on a group hiking trip. I was in Israel, on my own, and this guy Richard was here visiting his folks. Well, I had bought some hashish from an old Arab guy in Jaffa, and this stuff was Grade 'A', blow-your-mind-out stuff! Richard got a little higher than he had wanted and asked me not to take him home yet. He couldn't face his parents stoned. So, we started to drive. Next thing we knew, we were out by the Dead Sea. The night was perfect to be outdoors, so, when Richard mellowed out, he called his folks and told them that we were going to camp out, and we'd be home the next day. Well, we had nothing. No camping gear, no water, no change of underwear, nothing. So we conked out on the shore of the sea and let me tell you- you've never seen such a sky in your life! There were a billion stars out, and the moon reflected them off the water. It was pitch black otherwise. I knew God was in this place. Of course, that was half hash-induced, half my soul talking. We passed out on the beach of the sea and woke up with the sunrise over the Jordanian hills. Since it was so early, we got in the car and looked for water. So we started to drive and found some water at

Ein Gedi, and continued to drive some more. We found the road we're on now and eventually the road we're going to take. It was so cool to be out here, we didn't want to leave."

"That *is* so cool," Glenn replied. "I'm in shock!"

The road they were expecting finally came into view about thirty minutes later. Glenn couldn't imagine how bad the new road would be, since forty-five minutes on their current road was aggravating enough. Much to his dismay, Glenn soon found out why the new road was worse. Not only was it dirt, but it wasn't even groomed, full of bumps and potholes. Glenn couldn't drive faster than twenty-five miles an hour for risk of breaking an axle.

No sooner did he think about breaking an axle, it actually happened. Even at that slow speed Glenn didn't see it coming. The car's left tire found a foot-deep pothole that violently jolted the passengers inside the car. The vehicle came to such a forceful stop that Yossi flew into the windshield. He reacted fast enough for his wrists to take the brunt of the impact instead of his skull. Chayim and Avner, previously in the back seat thrust headlong into the front seat.

As quick as it happened, it was over. The four stayed in their positions, stunned over what had just occurred. Silence.

"Anyone dead?" Avner asked.

"My hands are," Yossi said, holding his hands up in the air. Both his wrists were starting to swell up like balloons.

"Jesus Christ!" Glenn screamed out when he saw Yossi's hands. A two-ton weight of guilt fell on him. "I am so sorry!" His voice quivered.

In his usual manner, Yossi replied without emotion. "Glenn, I didn't tell you the rest of the story. Remember I said we didn't want to leave when we found this place? Well, that was only *half* the story. True, it was beautiful out here. But the other part of the story is that we *couldn't* leave here. When I drove onto this road, I found a hole deeper than the one you just found. Same left side, same axle." Yossi was smiling in spite of the pain.

"But look at your hands!" Glenn pleaded, feeling like Yossi was letting him off the hook too easily.

"Something tells me that my broken hands are part of the play. We just have to act it all out. I know we're on the right track. This whole episode is bringing my life, both lives- from back then to the present- together! My old life has just revealed its purpose- this was *supposed* to happen to me! Don't you see? The Almighty has just brought my life full-circle! We're going on this trip for a very important purpose, and my old life is what brought me here now. Please, Glenn, you have to see that. Don't feel bad for what happened. It was my destiny!"

Glenn stared at Yossi straight in the eyes. He didn't blink, realizing Yossi was dead serious. Yossi convinced him that he truly wasn't responsible. Glenn managed to smile, but still felt like shit.

20

Everyone was slow to move but managed to stumble out of the car to inspect the damage. The front left wheel was nearly severed from the rusty axle. A car in better condition would likely have hit the pothole without incident, but this was an old car owned by a poor school. It had no chance.

"I guess we're walking the rest of the way," announced Avner, stating the obvious.

"Let's check the provisions in the trunk, said Yossi. "Just to make sure that I packed everything in my sleep-deprived state. If I did, then we'll have a lot to carry, but we'll be able to explore a little without having to hike back to the main road."

Avner opened the trunk and inspected its contents. It contained four sleeping bags, a blue five-gallon plastic container filled with water, three boxes of non-perishable foods such as potato chips, candy bars, and six large boxes of lasagna noodles.

"Lasagna noodles?" asked Chayim when he picked up a box of noodles.

"I took whatever I found in the kitchen. There wasn't much," said Yossi defensively.

"Can I ask you a question?" Avner chimed in. "How are we going to *cook* the noodles?"

"We aren't *going* to cook them, just eat them raw. Hey, next time *you* can prepare the food. I don't need the grief and I didn't see *you* volunteering to make sure we had something to eat!"

Glenn looked over everything that they had. "It's going to have to be up to the three of us to take turns carrying the water. That thing must weigh fifty pounds. There's no way Yossi can help with his sprained hands."

"Now that we're on foot, we actually can take a shortcut," Yossi announced. "The road only goes south but the hike eventually takes us west, away from the road. From here, we can weave in between the hills and head in a southwesterly direction. I'd say we're about nine miles from where I thought we'd start looking for the trail. Who knows? Maybe we'll find what we're looking for in just a mile."

Chayim volunteered himself and Glenn to carry the water first. Glenn didn't object. He moved over to the container and, together, he and Chayim lifted it. With this arrangement, the container wasn't heavy, just awkward. It was going to be a long walk with the bulky object. Avner and Yossi grabbed backpacks and stuffed them with the food. They elected to leave the sleeping bags in the car. If they were going to be outside overnight, they really didn't need the warmth of the sleeping bags anyway.

Everyone was carrying a fair amount of supplies, and the sun started baking as it rose higher into the morning sky. Even in the morning the heat of the Judean Desert in summertime was near scorching.

With no other option, the group journeyed to a place known only by one, and whether that place was close or miles away, no one knew.

21

As expected, the path was rugged and difficult to walk. Chayim and Glenn clumsily carried the water container while Avner and Yossi carried backpacks filled with food. Not even the heat deterred the yeshiva students from wearing the traditional black pants, white shirt, and undershirt with fringes on its corners. Only Glenn appeared to be dressed for the occasion wearing the same clothes he'd worn on the flight; khaki shorts and a t-shirt.

Though fatigued, none of them complained. All were well aware of just how important this journey was and the implications weighed heavily on their minds. Was the re-emergence of the Staff a harbinger of humankind's redemption or destruction? It was difficult to say which was the greater burden- the stress of uncertainty or the weight of the supplies they were physically carrying.

Conserving their energy with silence, the group maintained a slow but steady pace through the rocky terrain. There was not enough moisture for clouds to gather this time of year, and thus no relief from the relentless sun.

The four had advanced about three miles from the car when Yossi suggested that they take a break. "We actually should have stopped a while ago, so as not to become fatigued too early," he said.

"Hey- I think we may be even," winced Chayim, wringing his hands. "My wrists are in as bad a shape as yours from holding the water in such an awkward position. I think I've got carpel tunnel now."

After he shook off the pain, Chayim opened the container and poured the warm water into some paper cups that he pulled from one of the backpacks. Each of them gulped down the liquid and passed the cups back for a second round and then a third. Avner started to go for a fourth.

"Hey, go easy on the well," ordered Chayim. "We don't know how long we're going to be out here. Ration!"

"Are we even headed in the right direction?" asked Glenn. I'd hate the thought of lugging this thing around if we're not."

"Nobody knows what the 'right' direction is," Yossi calmly returned, "but if you're wondering if we're headed to the place that I'm thinking about then yes, we are. Absolutely."

The fifteen-minute rest passed by quickly. No one spoke and the silence was relaxing. Finally, Yossi piped up. "Okay," he breathed out heavily, "we need to get going."

The foursome gathered their belongings. Chayim half hoped that the round of drinks they all had would have made the water lighter to carry. But, for the size of the container, the amount of water they consumed was very little. It was still quite heavy.

The sun was nearing its zenith, and the heat almost unbearable. Each member of the group privately worked out their doubts about the whole thing, and whether they were crazy for taking it seriously. The fact that they were traveling in a direction based completely on a hunch did nothing to dispel the notion. If arriving at their destination was guaranteed, the trek would be much more tolerable. But now, as exhaustion set in, the idea of looking for the famous Staff of Moses in the desert wasteland sounded more and more like a storyline of some fantasy novel. On foot, without the convenience of a car, the whole idea began to feel more and more absurd. Though their faith was being tested, not one of them lost it.

Yossi began to recognize familiar surroundings. He recalled his time spent in these very hills, not all that long ago, amusing himself with what he used to come here for. Those were fun times indeed, however stupid. Even back then, when he was as high as a kite, he found undeniable spirituality here in this historical desert. He remembered feeling guilty at times, thinking this was, in essence, holy ground, and getting high here was bringing sacrilege to it. But now, he just knew, even his actions of old were for the greater good and those memories had brought him back here for a different and significant purpose. Everything felt right for him to begin the search here. What was to come of it, he did not know.

An hour at a time they would walk, take a ten minute break, and drink. The yeshiva boys removed their fringed undergarments, dampened them with the water, and wrapped them around their heads to protect them from the sweltering sun. Glenn used his shirt. He was already tan, so the chances of getting a sunburn at the low altitude of the desert was small. Soon, the water jug was only two-thirds its original volume.

By late afternoon, the group estimated how much ground they covered. Avner noticed a grin emerging on Yossi's face, marking surprised satisfaction.

"You're either seeing a mirage, have heat stroke, or you know something we don't."

"I know something you don't."

"You going tell us, or just stand there looking autistic?"

"See that ridge over there?" Yossi was pointing due south excitedly. "It's just over that ridge! I think it may have been easier to get here *without* a car. We're just about a mile from our target area!"

"That makes me happy," Chayim said hollowly. "It really does. But why do I only feel good about it and not great?"

"Because," answered Glenn, "we really don't really have a plan after we get there. This all may be a fruitless effort. And if it is, guess what? We get to walk all the way back out. That's the part that's going to piss me off."

After regrouping a few minutes, the group started back up, albeit a little more upbeat. Glenn felt like singing, and began to sing the first song that came into his head. He briefly wondered why this specific song came first. All their talk about religion might have had something to do with it. The song was a tune one might hear in a Baptist church down in the Bayou, and the lyrics were appropriate. "Sheep, sheep don't you know the Lord? Yeah, yeah, I know the Lord". Nobody would have minded him singing it if he hadn't repeated it at least fifty times. When round fifty-one kicked in Chayim made his feelings known.

"Sing that one more time and I'll kill you as you sleep."

Glenn muffled a laugh. The whole exchange brought a little levity, and was just what they all needed.

Avner wanted in. "I've got one!" He sang at the top of his lungs, "Drop kick me Jesus through the goal post of life, goal post of life, goal post of life." They all joined in for a chorus of 'Drop Kick Me Jesus' at least a dozen times.

"Nice. How 'bout this one?" Chayim contributed Weird Al Yankovic's satire to 'Cats in the Cradle'. "Did you ever think when you eat Chinese, it ain't pork or chicken but a fat Siamese..." Surprisingly, Glenn knew all the lyrics and joined in.

"There's a cat in the kettle at the Peking Moon, I gotta stop eating there at noon." Yossi and Avner only smiled as they moved their heads back and forth in musical rhythm.

Yossi couldn't resist. He continued with another of Yankovic's tunes, *"What If God Smoked Cannabis?"* This selection was particularly amusing.

"I'm hungry," Glenn admitted as he stopped walking, "let's take a break and eat some lasagna."

He sat his end of the water jug down on the ground and opened a backpack containing the boxes of the crisp noodles. He grabbed a noodle and began crunching away as he handed a few pieces to the others. All followed suit. He had to admit that the noodles actually tasted good raw, though crunchy. Feeling a bit jovial from the singing, Glenn's clown-like personality kicked in. He put his fingernails to his teeth as if going to bite them. And with a piece of crisp lasagna noodle in his mouth, he started crunching the noodle while pretending that he was biting his nails. That action was found particularly amusing by Yossi which caused him to blurt out a snorted, uncontrolled laughter. The problem was, he was swallowing during the process. After a quick couple of heaves, he dislodged the bolus and resumed chuckling. He wiped his eyes from the tears of laughter.

Fifteen minutes later they resumed their march and the singing continued. They progressed from silly lyrics to those they knew well from childhood- 'Row-Row-Row Your Boat' and the like. They sang for a long time, keeping their minds engaged as they approached the ridge pointed out earlier by Yossi.

The final three-hundred yards required to get there were extremely tedious. Sand filled the gaps between rocks adding a most challenging element to the walk. As the ridge turned into mountain, Yossi realized he had underestimated the difficulty of their route. He had never come from this direction before. Whatever hiking he did in his earlier day was from the access road, on trails paved by previous hikers and surveyors. In fact, it didn't appear as if anyone had traveled this way, at least not recently.

One hundred yards remained and the ridge looked less accessible than ever. Glenn was still singing, although the rest had dropped out, mostly because he was singing his own songs and no one else knew the words. The mood was no longer jovial, as the group recognized the trail ahead was steep and rocky. Looking to the top, Chayim had a foreboding feeling. He was carrying the water jug with Avner. Yossi's wrists weren't as swollen, but he still had limited ability to grip much. Chayim didn't complain, but the blister that had recently formed from carrying the water was now bleeding and burning. He ripped a piece of his dried undershirt that had covered his head to dress the blister.

Fifty yards with a slight incline lie ahead before the rocky ridge. It wasn't much, but enough of a psychological barrier to halt the troupe.

"Let's stop here," Yossi suggested. "There's no point in getting right on the ridge to stop. Besides, there's a better vantage point from this angle and we might be able to spot an easier way in."

They all dropped their stuff, fatigued from the journey. Avner looked on as Chayim unwrapped the bandage from his blistered hand. Avner wanted to convey some sympathy, but no words came. Everyone shared the same feeling. They were a team and one person's pain was the others as well. Chayim saw Avner's look of concern and returned with a thankful smile.

Yossi surveyed the ridge as they all drank water, moistened their head coverings and ate a ration of the food. The ridge wasn't exceptionally high, but at this point it appeared as daunting as Mount Everest to them. "It looks as if we can't get to the other side very easily from this point," he said. "I'm used to coming in-"

"What is that?" Chayim interrupted Yossi in mid sentence. He was looking up toward the ridge's peak about two-hundred yards away from their position. They all shifted their attention in the direction of where Chayim was staring, transfixed.

Glenn saw the object of Chayim's gaze. "Chayim, it's just a frickin bird. As long as it isn't a vulture, what are you so freaked-"

"It's a dove!" Chayim cried out.

"The desert's sucked out your senses. You're seeing things," retorted Glenn. "You're just *hoping* that it's a dove. Look at how it's circling. It's a hawk or something like that searching for food."

Avner was shaking his head. "No it's not. It's not a hawk or a bird of prey. Hawks circle like that, but they stretch their wings out while they circle. It's less movement of their bodies while they look on the ground for rabbits and stuff. This bird's flapping its wings."

Glenn admitted Avner was correct. This bird circled, but it didn't appear to be interested in hunting the desert floor. It just flapped its wings as it swirled around, making a big, one hundred foot circle in the air. If it were a hawk, it would have been the smallest and whitest hawk he'd ever seen. Even from afar, the bird appeared as white as snow.

They all looked in astonishment at each other. Adrenaline started its travels through each of their veins. The mountain that Yossi had camped at years ago was indeed the location of the Staff. The excitement motivated them to gather their belongings for the ascent to the top of the ridge. If the bird was a dove then what awaited them was nothing short of Heavenly. This was their invitation to advance toward the mysterious bird.

As Glenn walked toward their destiny he made a vow to himself to enroll in the yeshiva when they got back to Jerusalem. This was big. He started to feel it from the inside out and was trembling.

22

Heat and exhaustion were far from their minds as they watched, mesmerized by the white bird in flight.

Glenn remembered the words they read the night before from the Codex; *"The white dove will be seen at the time of danger and the time of redemption"*. This whole episode was becoming more and more surreal.

Halfway to their destination, the rocks of the ridge formed a U-turn, making an alcove-like crevice which created a three walled area that protected them from the sun and wind. But due to the difficulty of the terrain to get there, it had remained virtually intrusion-free. From this point, the rest of the way to the top was more accessible by foot than the first third of the ascent.

They entered the 'alcove' and stopped to look at their options. The spot, Yossi thought, would be a perfect place to camp or inhabit for a while, if one had to call the Negev Desert home. Shrubbery was also present which indicated the presence of an underground water source.

The view to the top of the ridge was extremely limited, but the bird circling overhead was an omen to the foursome that they were in the right place. Unless they opted to back track, there was nowhere in the crevice to go except upward. The group hesitated and then realized that, though steep, the rock face was less formidable here.

"Well, what are we waiting for?" Chayim announced. "Let's go."

"If you don't mind," Avner responded, "We've just been invited by God Himself to this spot. The least we can do is acknowledge that. I'm going to pray."

Chayim knew Avner was right, and was ashamed he didn't think to do the same, though the amount of adrenaline pumping through him would affect anyone's judgment. *But*, he also thought, this call from God may be the spark that will ignite mass destruction and could possibly be the initial end of the Earth. The situation, albeit divinely commanded, didn't necessarily imply fire and brimstone. The Codex had said that. But for which occasion the dove was allowed to be seen now no one knew, and that unknown weighed heavily on them all.

They all stood and faced toward Jerusalem and began the traditional afternoon prayer. Though he didn't remember any of the Hebrew words, Glenn stood facing toward the holy city, and started his own dialogue with God.

*   *   *

Ten minutes later they concluded praying, ready to perform the task at hand with the proper frame of mind. The sun had advanced westward enough to keep them in the shade for the climb. The boys dropped all of their belongings and corralled near the virtually depleted water jug for one final drink. Whatever was to become of them, their survival from this point onward was in the hands of their Creator.

No one spoke as they began the final ascent. Though in the shade, the air temperature was still extreme. Just about two hundred feet to go, in the searing desert heat, with no more water, all maintained their silence. As they scaled the mountain each continued to be cognizant of their reality; the broken car axle, the bird, the shaded crevice, the climb, and the call to each of them by God. The last of these was the most difficult to comprehend. They were actually a part of a call from the Creator; a call that had not occurred in over two-thousand years. And yet, here they were.

23

It took the foursome just under a half an hour to reach the top of the ridge. Out of water, they knew that they were to either die here or find hydration somehow. Each one of them valiantly accepted that fate in their heart. The foreboding events and their impact on the rest of the world weighed heavily on them. If the Codex was true, and they knew it was, then either redemption or annihilation was imminent. Peace would manifest either way, but that didn't mean that it would without terrible consequences.

"You can see everything from up here," Glenn spoke breathlessly from both appreciation and the hike.

"It's so desolate," Chayim added. "It's almost as if we're in a land and time all its own." It was true. Nothing manmade was in sight. The dove was perched atop a large rock attracting the attention of the sojourners.

It was the most beautiful bird they had ever seen, resting peacefully on a moss-covered rock that produced a blue-greenish hue. The group moved closer, fully expecting the dove to fly away. But it did not. It remained perfectly still on the green boulder.

"It sure is a long way to anywhere from here," Yossi remarked, stating the obvious. "Without any water, I mean."

"Check out the moss on this rock," said Avner as he glided his hand over the crusty surface. "How could moss grow all the way up here, at the top of a mountain? And why in just this two meter area?"

Yossi's exhaustion quickly triggered a frustrated response. "What do you mean 'why'? The dove sat down here as if to bring us to this very spot. And you're asking 'why'? The 'whys' and 'hows' don't matter here! It's the 'where' we need to determine. Start looking around. Maybe the dove will indicate if we're getting 'warmer' or 'cooler' with some sort of signal."

Chayim looked to see if the bird was providing any indication, when he noticed it was no longer sitting on top of the rocks. He looked around to see where it had flown, but it was completely out of sight. From this vantage point, it was impossible to miss it.

"Where is it?" Chayim asked.

"Where's what?" Glenn replied from inspecting the mossy rock.

"The dove!"

The four each scanned their immediate surroundings for anything that moved or was white. They found nothing.

"That bird was not from this world," Chayim announced with conviction. He stated what they all knew to be true. Obviously, the bird was not a figment of their collective imagination or a mirage. They had all witnessed it.

More important than finding the whereabouts of the dove, they had to determine why this particular spot had caught their attention. It wasn't exactly well hidden. Perhaps, they surmised, the best hiding place is out in the open.

Glenn continued to examine the moss on the rocks. "Typically, you would see moss from the ground level up," he informed the group, scouring over the material as they looked on. "Moss grows in damp, shady places. But the top of a ridge in the bright sunlight of a blazing desert is neither damp nor shady." Glenn spoke as if he were a geology professor on a field-trip with his students. He derived great satisfaction from telling people something they had not previously known. He was very intelligent and his college studies were wide and varied; simultaneously problematic and beneficial. Though he acquired a broad knowledge-base of interesting subjects, he simply wasn't focused enough to fully commit himself to one thing at the expense of learning about another. Consequently, he knew a little about a lot of things that didn't necessarily translate well into a traditional vocation. Eventually, his music, particularly his lyrics, depicted the opus of his life, and thus came to the forefront after the college years had passed.

"Notice too that this moss is only on a very little section of rock." Glenn kept up with his scientific observation, inspecting the edge of moss in relation to the rock, looking for a possible reason to why this growth was so unique. With the keys to the car in his pocket, he took them out and began to scratch away at the base of the rock. The moss flaked away with a little effort. Underneath, the moss revealed nothing more than the stone it had grown on. The rest of the group each studied a section of growth clues.

Yielding no new evidence, Avner discontinued using the credit card from his wallet to scrape away at the growth. He continued searching the rock for anomalies, but discovered nothing remarkable. Nothing, that was, except for a curiously darker section of moss at the base of the rock around eight square inches. He crawled to an area about five feet from where he was working to examine the section up close. The green color here was deeper by several shades from the section adjacent to it. Avner took the credit card and scraped away at this new section. The moss here was thick and clung tenaciously to the rock base.

"Hey Glenn, let me see those keys a second," he announced. Glenn walked over with the keys and handed them to Avner.

"What are you looking at?" Chayim asked as he approached the rest of the group.

"I'm not quite sure yet," answered Avner poking away at the material, "but it's different than what we're seeing anywhere else. Look at the deeper tone. I wonder if it means there's a water source here. That would certainly be a reason why there's moss up here and nowhere else."

He continued to scrape while the others looked on. The small scope of this area wouldn't allow for anyone else to assist. They merely stood by and waited.

Glenn surveyed the desert's landscape. It was stunning, to be sure, but it was so barren. It reminded him of their dire situation regarding water. He looked for miles around to see if any tree growth was nearby. He could barely make out the Dead Sea in the distance. Trying to remain optimistic, he supposed there was a chance they could walk that distance to get water, if necessary. Casting his gaze further to the right, he happened to notice a group of Bedouins heading south. Six in total, two of them were on donkeys.

"Hey guys, I see a group of Bedouins down by the road. I'll bet they'd sell us some water and fruit."

Chayim nonchalantly nodded toward Glenn, and returned his attention to Avner. His scraping had made some progress. "Check this out," Avner said in astonishment.

Yossi took his glasses off to examine the rock, and stuck his face within inches of the uncovered spot.

"This isn't calcium aluminum silicate. That would be the only type of blue-green rock in the Negev. Even then, to be found so far from the Dead Sea, which is filled with minerals, doesn't make sense. The Dead Sea is the closest, but it doesn't deposit calcium aluminum silicate in amounts like this, especially this high off the ground. Dig away some more- let's see how much there is."

"How do you know about 'calcium aluminum silicate'?" asked Glenn. "You said that like you knew what you were talking about."

"I don't want to talk about it."

Glenn looked again at Yossi with wondering eyes.

The four resumed their tedious scraping and examination, brushing away at the surface rock while ignoring the heat, thirst and exhaustion. After much effort, the four had uncovered only an inch or two more of the bluish stone. They found no more. But Glenn took notice of edges to the large stone and not just a slab of the larger rock that composed the ridge.

"Look! The blue-green stone led the way to this crack. Avner, give me that credit card a second."

Avner handed the card to Glenn. The use of the credit card as a tool had eliminated the ability to use it in its normal fashion. Glenn took the card and cut away moss that covered the crack. To their astonishment, as more and more moss was removed, the crack was revealed to go upward to the height of an average sized man, then arch over about three feet and then downward. The stone was a doorway.

Immediately they all took to widening the crack as much as they could to enable them to gain a grip on the edges to move it. Over time, their fingers became bloody from the scrapes incurred as they managed to scrape away moss and loose rock to gain a finger's width gap between the doorway stone and the ridge.

Hearts beating heavily from exertion and excitement, they all knew what was behind the rock.

Finally, Avner could not contain the emotion and started balling like a baby. In response to his sudden loss of control, the others managed to choke down their cries, but tears betrayed them in the hot afternoon sun.

They worked a piece of stone that had an edge thin enough into the space to try and wedge the rock away from its resting place. It gave a quarter of an inch, which was enough to drive the stone further in. Everyone pushed on the make-shift lever, moving the rock a bit more. Yossi's hands were completely swollen again. Little by little they made progress. Whenever it caught the sun's rays directly, the stone glistened like a jewel. Slowly, the space from the rock face became large enough for Chayim to peer into the crack. He could see the rock was obscuring the opening of a cave. Though it was too dark to determine how deep the cave was, the group knew it didn't have to be that big to contain the Holy Staff which they were certain was inside. Unearthing the cave made them more determined than ever. With two pushing the rock from one side and the other two pulling it, the foursome managed to move the rock another eight inches to make the opening large enough for at least one of them to tightly squeeze through.

"Who's the skinniest?" Glenn asked, looking at his stomach, sadly noticing the weight he'd put on over the last year. He ate a lot to soothe the stress of New York City and even more when his musical mental block set in. The increased caloric intake and lack of exercise had put fifteen pounds on him in a little over a year.

Chayim offered, "I am, but if Yossi can get in, I think he's the one who should go in first. If we're not all dreaming the same dream right now, we're about to witness the holiest artifact in the world. And Yossi's past that ultimately brought us here makes him the obvious choice to be the first to lay eyes on the Staff." Glenn and Avner nodded in agreement.

Yossi was trembling as guilt filtered into his mind. Why him? Of all the many righteous people in the world, why was *he* chosen, along with his trio of friends, for this task? These were questions that would never be answered.

Before attempting to enter through the small opening, Yossi knelt down and meditated. Avner and Chayim joined in, and so did Glenn, though he didn't really know what to say; so he made up his own prayers. The words stirred his soul.

Five minutes later, Yossi stuck his head into the opening. Avner and Glenn each grabbed a foot and helped push Yossi in. Yossi's shirt caught the rock, but the momentum managed to keep him moving inwards. Yossi wiggled his way in. The group eagerly waited for a report from outside the cave, but none was given. A few anxious moments later, Glenn asked outright for a report.

"Yossi...come on already! What do you see?"

A sound of muffled crying emerged.

"Yossi," Chayim called out as calmly as his trembling voice allowed. "Please, buddy. Please tell us what you see."

The boys waited outside while they waited for Yossi to compose himself. Finally, he managed to choke out the words, "There's a *man* in here!"

24

"What do you mean?" Avner yelled into the cave. "Do you mean a skeleton?"

"No, I don't. There is a man in here," Yossi replied stoically.

"Can we talk to him?" Glenn asked.

"He's not alive," Yossi replied. "It looks as though he just died."

The three outside looked at each other in disbelief. Even if this cave had been perfectly sealed for as long as they knew it had, decomposition would be inevitable. They were hearing the impossible.

"If it's a sin," Glenn said as he took position by the rock, "God forgive me but I've *got* to see this. Yossi, is there enough space for anyone else to go in?"

"Yes, in fact you all can actually."

Avner and Chayim also nodded to each other that this was something to be seen. Each one squeezed through the hole into the cave, even Glenn who sucked in his gut in order to keep from having to widen the opening. It took several moments for their eyes to adjust to the darkness but after a few minutes, they were able to recognize the shape of a body, confirming what Yossi had said. There, before them, was a man lying below a mantle with his eyes closed and just as Yossi said, as though he had just died moments earlier.

*   *   *

    In the dim light, they strained to see his face, his clothes, or anything that might give them a clue as to who he was. This discovery would surely make them all rich; an archeologist's dream. Wealth, however, was the last thing on their minds. The man was dressed in ancient garments that appeared to be from around the first to second century, A.D. Contrary to his dress, everything about the man was relatively fresh; he was approximately twenty-five years old, with sandals still on his feet and in good shape, as was the white tunic on his head.   His legs had lines of dried blood from scratches that covered both his ankles. His handsome face was pale white and there were no signs of decomposition anywhere. Truly, he looked as though he were sleeping.   Though he appeared to be recently deceased, they knew this was not possible, for the cave had been sealed for centuries.

    "He must have been the one to bring the Staff here," Chayim finally announced. It was then that

Avner drew everyone's attention to a crevice in the rock wall. There, in the darkness of the cave, a shroud was placed upon the mantle. Nervously, Yossi removed the shroud from its resting place and slowly unwrapped it, careful not to tear the brittle cloth.

"This cloth has got to be thousands of years old," Yossi said. His hands were quivering. He removed the last piece of cloth, revealing the awesome sight of The Holy Staff. Yossi rapidly murmured prayers to himself as he put his hands around the Staff. He brought it into view for his friends to see. It was just as the writings had described it; roughly two yards long, with an inscription written in ancient Hebrew on its side. A beautiful gem, probably sapphire, inlaid into the Staff's top third, glimmered softly in the dim light.

"Oh my goodness," mumbled Glenn. "Do you realize what you have in your hands?"

Avner allowed the moment to soak into his soul. "The Staff of Moses... created from the wood of the original Tree of Life, in the Garden of Eden," he recited just loud enough for them all to hear. His mind continued to work, to fully comprehend the object before them. "This Staff was held by Adam, Noah, Abraham, Isaac and Jacob, and eventually given to Moses. And now I'm actually touching it," he said as he ran his fingers lightly over its polished surface. "Moses took this Staff up to Mount Sinai when he got the law from God Himself." His head shook slowly in disbelief.

Yossi bent down with the Staff to the dead man. "Thank you," he whispered. "Your mission was successful. And your holiness kept you from becoming dust of the ground." Yossi touched the corpse's shoulder. "Please ask the Creator to give us the strength to succeed in our mission now!"

Avner chanted the prayer for the dead, and all stood over the man they never knew. They paid their last respects to him, and then Yossi took the Staff and re-wrapped it for their continued quest, of which they had no idea where to go from here.

Glenn exited the cave first, followed by Avner and Chayim. Yossi held onto the Staff and waited for someone outside to receive it before he climbed out. He extended the Staff to a hand waiting in the opening. When he finally emerged from the cave he saw the others were surrounded by a band of six Bedouin men, each with a rifle pointed straight at their heads.

25

"Thank you very much, gentlemen," the voice sneered triumphantly in Hebrew with a thick Middle-Eastern accent. "On behalf of the honorable Mohsen Pandseh, we convey our heartfelt thanks for your efforts in retrieving The Holy Staff," he continued acidly. His was the arm that had reached into the cave, retrieving it from the unsuspecting Yossi.

Glenn gawked at the men around him, pointing rifles at his head. This couldn't be happening. He felt like it was made up, as if he were an actor in an action movie, and this was all part of some script he hadn't rehearsed. His mind slowly woke up to the reality, telling him this was no movie; these were real men, real enemies pointing real rifles at them... and ready to kill them.

Yossi thought about the words in the Codex. *'The white dove will be seen at the time of danger and the time of redemption. Man will not know which it is'.* It was becoming apparent which outcome was unfolding.

Glenn was paralyzed as the sniper spoke, but he didn't understand a word. Questions raced through his mind: how did these men know about the Staff? Who were they? If God wanted someone else to ultimately have the Staff, why were they chosen to find it? Why the dreams? The trip all the way to Israel? He thought of his parents who had no inkling their son was anywhere short of a nice vacation in Israel.

"Who are you?" Glenn challenged in English. He was scared to hear the answer. He thought about Chayim, whose mother would be devastated if something were to happen to him. The gravity of it all started to press down on him.

"Oh, you are American?" the leader replied, this time in English. "It is not important who I am. But I am glad to know that you are an American. Are all of you Americans?"

"Yes," was Avner's immediate response. "We all are." He was hoping their American status might diffuse the situation, if only a little. At this point, being American was better than being an Israeli. Dressed in their black pants, beards, and head coverings, they were instantly associated with the 'Occupiers'.

"Ah. You are on vacation?"

"Yeah. We just went camping for a couple of days," Avner replied as casually as he could. He prayed his words came across sincerely.

"I see. And where are your supplies?" Surely you must have water. You do look a bit thirsty. Did you all forget them at your campsite? Where is your campsite anyway?" The man's patronizing tone revealed he was on to their game.

Chayim sensed who the men were. "You followed us, but you're not Bedouins, are you?"

"Correct," replied the leader. "We are Iranian nationals paying a visit to this wonderful country." He hesitated and raised his hand to take back what he had just said. "I'm sorry, we're paying a visit to *our* wonderful country. *You* are in Muslim territory... illegally! *You*, and all the millions like you who occupy this land. But that is a different matter. Your position was extremely easy for us to follow. Thank you for flashing the mirror for all to see."

Glenn shivered as he remembered- the blue-green stone did indeed flash like a mirror. Caught up in all the excitement, they had inadvertently given away the secret location of the Staff and had led these men right to it. Glenn was baffled why God would intend for this to happen and grew angry thinking about the injustice of it all.

"You will come with us. At least some of you will. We cannot risk the chance of getting out of your pathetic country with such a large group." Without so much as a second passing by since the end of his sentence the leader quickly turned around and shot Yossi and Avner square in the middle of their chests. The two dropped to the ground with the looks of shock sewn permanently into their faces. The terrorists provided no opportunities for them to plead for their lives, let alone say goodbye to their friends. Chayim howled as his companions dropped by his side. He and Glenn looked on, helplessly, at Avner and Yossi, then fearing their own demise. Their lives were in the hands of someone with an agenda, just waiting for the right time to shoot them dead after they had fulfilled their unknown purpose. Two of the Iranians picked up the bodies and shoved them into the cave. The leader pointed his gun in the direction of Glenn and Chayim while the others all pushed the main stone back into its original position in front of the cave entrance. They moved additional stones in front of the main boulder to ensure extra effort would be required to retrieve the bodies... that is, if anyone even knew of their whereabouts.

The leader spoke stoically as only a heartless killer could, "You will come with us, please, for both our sakes."

Glenn and Chayim moved with their captors down the rock side, wailing in dismay for their friends and for the future.

26
Tehran, Iran

Mohsen sat in the humidity-controlled room smiling like a little boy with a new toy. He just stared at the Staff, absorbing all that this artifact meant and the rich history associated with it. The Staff would be worth billions, if not priceless. It was the single most important artifact to come into man's grasp.

World knowledge of the Staff would be an igniter of faith. Those who believed already would only become more faithful. Those who lacked it would be faced with the reality that the Old Testament was true. It was indeed powerful in that sense. But neither the money nor the fame for finding the Staff was what Mohsen desired. This was a device used to communicate directly with God. The Staff contained powers instilled by God Himself, and Mohsen was anxious to see if he could tap into that efficacy.

He picked up the Staff, admiring once again its raw beauty. He wondered for a moment what part of the Staff Moses had held most often. The Staff showed absolutely no signs of wear and tear. Its wood showed no scratches or nicks. The Hebrew inscription, which he had yet to decipher, was very pronounced, considering the many hands that had touched it, the windblown sand of the desert that had undoubtedly beaten against it, not to mention its age. Everything about the Staff was in perfect condition, including the radiant sapphire gemstone inlaid in it which shone as brilliantly as if it were buffed that very morning.

Mohsen stood up from his chair wearing the latex gloves to remove the Staff from its wrapping. If he could just figure out *how* to use it, the potential it possessed would allow Mohsen to do anything. So many things he could do with the Ultimate Power, but one item in particular stood out in his mind. He wanted influence. To be the greatest Muslim ever known, second only to Mohammed, was his lifelong wish since he was a young adult. Emotion overcame Mohsen knowing that he had within his grasp the ability to make that happen.

First, he needed to learn how to use the power and thus, he needed to start off small. Staff in hand, he held onto it three quarters from the top with his right hand. He raised his hand up in the air and said in his native tongue, "Let there be a glass of water appear on this table!" Mohsen looked down at the table. The room didn't shake, thunder didn't rumble, and a glass of water did not appear. Nothing at all happened. He attempted the request again in broken Hebrew. Still nothing. He then decided that a request was not the way to make it work. He used a more stern approach this time. "I command a glass of water appear on this table... now!" Frustratingly, again nothing happened.

Afshin watched the whole thing on the closed circuit camera from an outside office. He was not allowed in the room while Mohsen delighted in his acquisition. Watching the antics of his half-crazed boss made Afshin laugh, for he knew the power of the Staff would not respond to anyone who happened to be in possession of it, making arbitrary demands. It was not that simple. He knew that Moses was a prophet. Only during a prophetic moment would commands be given to the Staff and for a response. The Staff alone was not the power. Rather, it was merely a conduit to the spiritual realm, and only through the prophetic state could it be retrieved.

He looked on at his boss with growing amusement, feeling superior over Mohsen who had been so controlling and belittling. Afshin walked casually over to the bar and poured himself a drink from a bottle with no label on it. He returned to the table next to the closed circuit monitor, setting his drink down, and continued to observe. A few moments later, predictable expletives spewed through the closed circuit speakers as Mohsen became frustrated from his failure to make the Staff work. He set it down on the table, and exploded into a violent tantrum, throwing papers and other desktop objects across the room. He slammed the door as he exited the room. Seconds later, Mohsen entered the outside office.

"You've been watching, no doubt."

"Yes. Why wouldn't I?"

"And you knew I wouldn't be able to get it to work, correct?" Mohsen saw the drink in Afshin's hand and decided that he could use one too. He motioned for Afshin to serve him.

"Of course," Afshin replied assuredly putting ice into a glass.

"So, what do I need to do- say *please*?" Mohsen asked, his vexation apparent. Afshin knew Mohsen was more disappointed over his loss of control. "Don't tell me I need the help of those Jewish kids."

"Okay, I won't tell you that," Afshin said. He was uncharacteristically relaxed.

"Play with me any longer, and I'll shove the Staff down your throat. The pleasure of seeing it being put to good use would more than make up for my inability to command it," Mohsen barked, feeling he was regaining some semblance of control.

Afshin acknowledged Mohsen. "Very well. Do you not understand that the power within the Staff is reserved for only a select few? Do you think anyone can simply pick it up, make a request and expect it to work?" Afshin was regaining the much desired control over his boss. "God is not stupid," he continued, "putting such power into a vehicle for ordinary men to play with. With a higher purpose in mind, man must make the ascent into the spiritual realm. He must *see* the next world, and then become part of it! Only then, will he have any chance for the spiritual to respond to him. The Staff is a conduit, not the object of power. One must understand this and humble himself if he is to succeed. Moses the prophet had this quality. He understood. And now, you must understand too."

Mohsen was indeed humbled, realizing Afshin was right. "Okay, then what must we do?" Using the term 'we' felt funny to him.

Afshin moved forward in his seat. "*We* must learn the ways to prophecy. I have books to start learning the basics. But that will only take us so far. At some point, we must actually practice the discipline."

Mohsen was disheartened. "But this is going to take a long time."

"Then, we must start at once."

Mohsen thought about the hostages his men had brought to him. "What about the Jews, then? Do we need them?"

"Not yet," Afshin answered. "If we run into any obstacles during our training we can use the educated one to get answers. We can kill the other if you wish."

Mohsen considered Glenn's fate for a moment before responding. "No. Even though no one knows their whereabouts, I am certain somebody else knows they went to the desert and why. When they don't return in the next few days, I am certain that concern will prompt a search for them. They should have killed him in the desert. Besides, once we're successful with the Staff, it won't matter. In the meantime, treat them well."

Afshin agreed. "We will allow them to e-mail home to say they're alright, ease any fears, and explain they're busy doing archeology digs. Of course, they will comply if they want to stay alive."

27

The view from the tenth floor of what appeared to be a high-rise condominium or apartment was stunning. Overlooking an affluent suburb of Tehran, one had an unobstructed view of the city from the condo's large floor-to-ceiling glass windows that ran continuously along two sides of the long corner unit. Their trip from the airport to the condo confirmed their location via the highway signs, many surprisingly in English inscribed under the Persian.

The large living room was over two thousand square feet and with wooden floors and high twenty-four foot ceilings. The room's contents boasted a lavish and eclectic décor of fine imports- art, sculptures, furniture and room accessories were professionally displayed. The kitchen was separated from the living room by a simple yet elegant island of maple cabinets below topped off with solid forest green granite tops and polished stainless steel gas stove and matching exhaust. The balance of kitchen appliances were also stainless steel and a complete set of shiny copper pots hung next to the exhaust. The balance of the condo's space was used up by two well sized bedrooms and a main guest bath. Both bedrooms contained their own bathrooms. Those too were tastefully designed and accessorized.

The condo was Mohsen's second home in the Tehran area. It was close to the central business district and downtown Tehran. He used it occasionally, attending to business in the city or when returning from or going on business trips. This location was much more convenient for getting to or from the airport as the commute was only ten minutes compared to the thirty-five minutes needed to get to his warehouse, which also boasted cozy and elegant living facilities. Moshen worked such long days, and oftentimes late into the night, that it only made sense to turn the upper portion of his warehouse facilities into living space as well.

Mohsen also used the condo when he was in need of female companionship. He didn't dare take any of the gold diggers, which served his physical needs, back to his warehouse. Single women looking to hook a rich fish would have melted upon seeing the contents of imports stored at the warehouse.

But despite the lavish accommodations, the condo was still a prison cell for Glenn and Chayim. They knew that the fate of their comrades, Yossi and Avner, could easily await them at any time and at any moment without warning. Additionally, they still hadn't met their captors, only the gorillas that were assigned to watch over them at the condo. Based on the rhetoric of the leader who had taken them hostage, they feared at the thought that their captors were extremists and had to continually fight off the horrible imagery of being executed via methods of the seventh century.

Chayim tried to keep focus on his faith, refusing to believe that God would allow the Staff to fall in the hands of a wide-eyed, fanatical lunatic. Perhaps God was merely watching from the sidelines and this whole expedition was an experiment to see if man's evil was stronger than his good. That thought brought on despair making it difficult not to wallow in. On the other hand, he thought, these may truly be the End of Days as prophesied in the Bible and though they would ultimately be for the greater good, dark days would surely test the faith of the entire world.

These thoughts raced through Chayim's mind like a freight train. He couldn't stop thinking about his mom and how devastated she would be if something were to happen to him. If she lost her son now she would surely give up the will to live and to him, the thought of this was worse than world destruction. He loved his mom dearly and missed her. Right now, she was probably wondering why he hadn't called lately and if he was okay. He wished he could call her just to let her know that he was alright.

Glenn too realized the gravity of the situation. Normally the optimist, he had a knack for making the best of bad situations. One time, for example, he was

playing at 'The Dugout' located on the upper east side
of Manhattan when the power went out in all the
microphones on stage. Two thousand people were in
attendance that night, including a girl he was very
interested in. Sensing the audience was growing
impatient with the repairs, Glenn began to play a song
on the piano. He soon got up from the piano and held
his hands to his ears, miming to the audience that he
couldn't hear them. The audience picked up the queue
and soon the entire house sang the song while the band
played. With a little time and an extra long
instrumental, the repairs to the mics were made and
the concert continued to everyone's satisfaction. The
next day's paper rated his performance as one of the
best in a small venue circuit.

But at this moment there was no room for
optimism. Glenn recognized the impact of the
developments on his life over the last few weeks and
how much more devoted he was going to try and become
to his faith. Then he scared himself. It was possible,
really possible, that he wouldn't have the chance to do
that. Though he believed in God, he couldn't
understand why God was allowing this to happen.

Chayim moved closer to Glenn who was sitting in
an accent chair facing a large window that overlooked a
beautiful suburb of Tehran. Glenn was lost in thought
as he stared out the window at nothing in particular.
Looking down to the streets, they noticed women
wearing burkas, covered from head to toe in modest
dress, and others wearing Al-Amira Hijabs which
covered their head and face.

Because they were in a residential area, Glenn initially surmised they were being held captive by a group of individuals and not the government. That brought little comfort, however. Even if they managed to escape, there was no United States Embassy in Iran. And, if they were to go to the government, they would likely be arrested and charged as spies since they were without a passport. Glenn was pretty sure that spies didn't fare very well in Iran.

Upon further consideration, Glenn thought it was possible these people were part of a government organization or that the government was indirectly involved. Either way, the prospects were grim. He wondered how he and Chayim were smuggled into the country with such ease.

"You okay?" Chayim finally asked.

"As well as could be expected, I guess," Glenn answered deflated, remaining fixed on the window. He shook his head slowly. "I can't believe he just shot Yossi and Avner like it was no big deal."

"These guys are used to violence. To them, we are enemies," Chayim replied.

"It's nothing short of crazy. Tell me something, what's your gut feeling about all this? What do you think God has in mind? He certainly seems to be allowing this to go on and it doesn't appear to be going our way. Is it all coming to a head? I mean, the whole fire and brimstone thing... you think it's time?"

"Very possibly. We will know the days of the messiah are here when the world falls into utter chaos.

And look at it. The world is so upside down. What's right is wrong and what's wrong is right."

Glenn mustered up a half smile, his spirits lifting slightly. "I've always loved to travel. And here I am in a foreign country. Before yesterday, it would have been the greatest thing. Now, I'm looking over a neighborhood in Iran and never in a million years would I have thought I'd be *here* of all places. This place is the center of controversy in the world today; the center of hatred toward Israel and the West. If this is part of God's plan, he sure is making it interesting."

Glenn returned his thoughts to their departed friends. "I can't believe Avner and Yossi are gone. Just like that. They may never even get a proper burial. Is that justice? What does our faith say about bad things happening to good people Chayim? There's no justice for them!"

"It's not God's justice." Chayim tried to reassure his friend. "You have to give God a chance."

"But, aren't you the least bit angry at God for taking Avner and Yossi?" Glenn asked anxiously.

"No," Chayim said, "I am not. How do we know if Avner and Yossi aren't in a better place than we are now? And if they are, who should be sad for whom? For all we know, they're looking down at us now, feeling sad that we're in the situation that *we're* in. Glenn, if our faith is correct, then that's how it really is. My sadness is not for them. They are in paradise. I'm sad for us! I have to live the rest of my life, however long or short that may be, without *them*. *That's* the hard part. My sadness is therefore purely selfish."

Glenn took Chayim's words to heart. "There you go again, Chayim. Where did you learn all this? That's incredible. It actually does make me feel better knowing that. I guess, if we die, it's a good thing then."

"Well, yes and no. As far as Avner and Yossi are concerned, I would absolutely say 'yes'. The one exception for me would be my mother. I couldn't bear to think how things might be if she ever heard I died and I just can't allow that happen."

"Yeah, I know what you mean. I'd really like to talk to my parents. Just to be able to tell them I'm alive. To tell them I love them."

"And you will have your chance my young friend," a voice startled them from behind. Glenn and Chayim spun around to see a short, well groomed man with dark facial features and a mustache listening in on their conversation.

"My American friends, my name is Mohsen Pandseh. Welcome to the beautiful city of Tehran. I am pleased to make your acquaintance."

The man spoke in perfect English. His slight accent was typical of the region.

"We are American citizens that you have taken away against our will," announced Glenn.

"I am perfectly aware of what we have done, young man," Mohsen answered both defiantly and calmly. "And if you wish to continue to live, I suggest you save your words for more constructive discussions."

Mohsen waited for a response but Glenn did not offer one, so he continued. "I too have a great love for the Staff. To hold the very channel which God performed so many miracles with is quite exciting, don't you agree?" Mohsen walked from the entryway and stood between the boys and the picture window. Taking in the view he said, "A lovely view, wouldn't you agree? I hope the accommodations have made your stay comfortable."

"Well, I don't feel exactly like I'm at the French Riviera, but it'll have to do," Glenn replied.

Mohsen smiled. "I love your sense of humor," he said genuinely. "Though I am not an overly religious person, I do understand the power that the Staff represents. I have some very specific needs which require its assistance. If you are patient, then all will be well and I will become the greatest Muslim that ever lived, except of course to the great Mohammed. Once I achieve my objective, I will send you on your way."

"It is difficult to be patient knowing our parents are probably worried from not having heard anything from us in days," Glenn said continuing the role of spokesman. He thought his fair skin and American clothing would be better received opposed to his friend who was still wearing his skullcap and fringes.

"I understand," replied Mohsen. "We will allow you to email home by the end of the day. The email will appear as though it's coming from Tel Aviv. You will assure your parents that you're having a great time, and that you've been invited to stay a while longer. You will be direct, using words from a script that everything is fine. Should you deviate from my direction, I guarantee your lives will end precisely at that moment.

You have my word that your cooperation will be reciprocated."

"Why should we believe you? What do you need from us anyway?" asked Glenn.

"You knew where to find the Staff," Mohsen replied, "and thus, you might know something that could help me put it to use. Until then, enjoy the accommodations I have arranged for you. Please feel free to ask one of my assistants and they will grant you access to most anything you wish. I will be back to check on you soon. So please, make yourselves at home."

Mohsen exited the condo, and left the door open behind him, allowing Chayim and Glenn to see him talking to one of his assistants. The dialogue lasted for a few minutes while they occasionally looked back at Chayim and Glenn. When the discussion was over Mohsen headed for the elevators to leave the building.

28

Two weeks had passed since Mohsen and Afshin began their training in meditation. Their goal was to achieve a portal of light from the spiritual world without losing consciousness. What came naturally to Afshin was a challenge to Mohsen who was uneasy about meditating in the first place. Simply 'letting go' did not come easy to someone who needed to feel like he was in complete control at all times.

To maximize their attempts at success, Mohsen converted a storeroom at his warehouse in the upstairs area into a comfortable meditation room. The room was large, but Mohsen had everything removed from it and had the walls padded to absorb any outside noises. The room was part of the larger and beautiful five thousand square foot office which included luxurious and cozy sleeping, bathing, recreational and kitchen accommodations as well. The two sat in the room on zafus, small black pads that were placed on the floor in the middle of the windowless room lit only by a thick white candle that sat on top of the room's only other accessory; a five foot long maple coffee table arranged between the zafus. The only other article in the room was the Staff, placed delicately on a new fresh shroud on the table and in closer proximity to Mohsen. Mohsen would not let it out of his site.

The pair trained according to a discipline Afshin had studied years ago at Tehran University. The two had just completed their latest two hour meditation training.

"How do you do it?" an exasperated Mohsen asked.

"Do what?" Afshin replied with a barely audible whisper, annoyed at the interruption. Though their meditation exercise was complete, Afshin needed time to acclimate from his relaxed state and the slightest noise was as deafening as thunder.

"I've watched you during training. You're almost there. I know it."

Afshin realized avoiding this conversation was futile. He forced himself to withdraw from the semi-coherent state he was in. "You are right. I actually have been making very good progress," he said. "I have to admit that the training I received at the University seems to be paying off now. Those disciplines are the keys to achieving our intention."

"It is hard to let go," Mohsen admitted.

"I more than understand, but to summon the power of the Staff you must release yourself from this world."

196 | Jeff Wedgle

"Ah, the power of the Staff!" Mohsen sighed with a wide grin as he tilted his head to look upward. "It is going to serve such wonderful purposes!" I need to focus on the power it contains. That will help me let go."

Afshin paused for a moment, waiting for Mohsen to list off what his intentions with the artifact were. When Mohsen did not continue, Afshin spoke up. "May I ask what you intend to do with the power, should you be successful?"

Mohsen snapped, "You mean *when* I become successful? You underestimate me my young friend. Have I not proved myself over and over again? What have I not achieved that I put my time and energy into?" Though it was obvious to his ego that Afshin's question did not deserve a reply, he searched for an answer anyway. "Though I am not sure how, I first intend to make every Muslim rich so that no Muslim will ever go without. That itself will be more than enough to make me what I intend to be- second only to Mohammed.

"Do you not want to destroy America? Or Israel? Do you not want to control Europe? What about the suffering of our brothers at the hands of the occupiers?"

"Their suffering will end when they have enough money in their pockets. They won't need that land. If all goes to plan, we will eventually take over Europe anyway, and by natural means. Let the Jews have the desert, leaving Jerusalem for us; they can have the rest. They will gradually be overtaken anyway. I intend to use the power in a way that appears as an ordinary course of events in the eyes of the world. I want to become great through as natural a process as possible."

"Yes, but the 'desert' you refer to is holy land! *Our* holy land. It must be liberated!"

"Yes, my devoted friend, but in time. Remember, money is the key to all happiness. With wealth, the people will not suffer, I can assure you- land or no land. In any event, we will resume training in a couple of hours. In the meantime, I need to eat. Meditation makes me hungry. I will be in the kitchen. I'll pay you for your lesson in meditation by making you a sandwich."

"I will join you shortly," Afshin replied, stifling his frustration with Mohsen's desired use of the Staff. "Will you trust me with the Staff for five minutes? I'd like to meditate just a few minutes more. I was beginning to get a vision."

"Fine," replied Mohsen with some concern. "Just bring the Staff when you're done. I do not want it out of my site."

Afshin nodded with eyes closed. Reassured, Mohsen rose from his mat, walked out of the meditation room and closed the door behind him. The candle was still burning in the dark, noiseless room. Afshin took some deep breaths, keeping his eyes closed and letting go of his thoughts. Soon, the desired ruminative state filtered back into his body.

Slowly, Afshin reached for the Staff and held it gently with both hands, fully immersed in concentration. The Staff's beautiful inlaid gem started to glow radiantly. Eyes closed and mind open, the

198 | Jeff Wedgle

ancient Hebrew words left his mouth. His command to the Staff was to stop the beating heart of Mohsen Pandseh.

If liberating the occupied land and destroying the Great Satan was not Mohsen's top priority, he would forfeit the right to execute his plan. His presence was no longer necessary to further the real cause.

As Afshin heard the faint screams of pain and the plea for help coming all the way from the kitchen, Afshin acknowledged Mohsen's contributions for getting the Staff into the hands of the holy. Then he said the prayer for the dead.

29

Afshin appeared helpless as he watched the medical team try to revive Mohsen in the kitchenette of the warehouse where he suffered his fatal heart attack. The medical team of three had arrived in a matter of minutes, but Moshen was completely unresponsive.

As Mohsen's body lie motionless on the ground, Afshin observed him, recalling the last two decades of loyal service. The reflection was bittersweet. Though Afshin knew it was time to end Mohsen's life, he couldn't help but become emotional over his death. And though it was time to close the book on this particular chapter of their lives together, Afshin reflected on their relationship and the many things he learned from his former boss during that time; the last of which was to use the Staff as stealthily and sparingly as possible. Afshin also knew that, even with the power of the Staff, he was not ·immortal and no matter how much protection it provided, he would still be vulnerable to the selfish hearts of men. There would be others that would come to cherish the awesome power that he now possessed, and they would stop at nothing to obtain it. Even Moses confronted evil men who wished to take his place, and Afshin would be no exception. For this he knew Mohsen was right- the Staff must be used selectively and silently.

"I am afraid there is nothing more that we can do sir," the lead paramedic informed Afshin, his thoughts jolted back into the present moment. "The damage to his heart appears to be too severe. The attack was massive, yet he does not appear to be in the poor conditions that are typical of most who suffer these types of trauma, though it does happen from time to time. I'm very sorry."

"This all just happened so fast that it is difficult to believe it actually happened," replied a stoic Afshin. "Mohsen has been my boss for twenty years. This just can't be happening."

"We are going to take the body for an official pronouncement of death. Sir, if it's not too hard on you, the medical examiner will want to ask you some questions. Just to rule out any foul play. This is standard procedure, I can assure you."

"No, that is fine. I understand. I will go with you. May I follow you in my own car?"

"Certainly, sir- that is no problem. The process will only take a few hours. A V.I.P. area is available which have private rooms for your comfort while waiting. I will see to it that you are most comfortable."

"Thank you," replied Afshin as he watched the stretcher being brought in. The medical team moved Mohsen's lifeless body onto the stretcher, placed a white sheet over him, and proceeded down the metal staircase that led from the upstairs offices to the main level below.

"I need to gather some things to take with me," Afshin informed the paramedic. "After I lock up, I'll pull my car around and will follow your lead."

"No problem," the paramedic replied. "Take your time. Sadly there is no hurry for your boss any longer."

Afshin felt a bit of detachment in the man's voice. He assumed the man had seen his fair share of death.

The medical team left through the main door as Afshin returned upstairs to retrieve the Staff. He walked down the hallway into the dimly lit meditation room. The Staff rested softly on top of a new shroud, supplied from the imported inventory of pure, silk fabric from Japan. The original covering lay beside it. Afshin observed the artifact as it sat innocuously on top of the silk. "*So apparently innocent, yet so powerful and deadly,*" he murmured.

Afshin wrapped the artifact in the new shroud and hurried back down the stairs. His eagerness to use the Staff was unbearable, but he maintained his own conclusion that all must be done to appear as natural as possible. It would have caused suspicion for Afshin to be away from his boss when the news agencies received news of Mohsen's passing.

As he went out to his car he was shocked that one news team had already gotten wind of Mohsen's death. A film crew was taping the scene of Mohsen being taken away by the paramedics. The Staff was placed gently in the back seat and Mohsen pulled the car around to wait behind the ambulance for the trip to the morgue.

*   *   *

Several more news trucks awaited the ambulance and Afshin's car as they pulled up to the morgue. It was shocking to see how quickly news travels and how ready the news agencies are in order to capture footage of Mohsen's body being taken out of the ambulance covered by the white sheet. In the fifteen minute commute to the morgue, the news agencies were not only notified of the death, they were parked and with cameras rolling as the ambulance pulled up. Lights from the cameras lit up the immediate area as the media stormed to get a story of the cause of death. Afshin accompanied the paramedics and entered the morgue without any comment for the reporters.

The private morgue appeared more like a hotel than a morgue. Families of its renowned clientele enjoyed private family rooms with full bathroom facilities and beds in a luxurious facility. The deceased were inspected and prepared in the basement by a full time staff responsible for watching over them until the burial. Mohsen's body was taken to the basement while

Afshin retired to a private bereavement room on the main floor, awaiting the medical examiner. The time was ten-thirty in the evening.

Once the media had left and all was quiet, Afshin quickly but stealthily went out to his car to retrieve the Staff. Once back in his room he immediately locked the door and set off to work. In the period of time it would take to inspect Mohsen's body, Afshin would be able to perform a few vital prerequisites necessary to execute his plan to disable all military threats while gaining control of all world media. No matter the vehicle, whether it was television, radio or even internet news, the eyes and ears of humanity would be forced to witness the execution of the sinful with their own eyes.

Afshin removed a pillow from the sofa and centered it on the floor. He removed his shoes and took the Staff from where it rested on the bed. He moved to the floor and postured himself to begin meditation. This time, however, was not easy for Afshin to concentrate. The very idea of him becoming the chosen prophet to do God's will greatly distracted him. What needed to happen would finally come to pass, and the excitement of knowing he would be the cause of it prevented him from focusing. As the hours rolled painfully and slowly into the night, he finally found the right mixture of concentration, relaxation and mindfulness enabling him to finally let go.

Once the trance was achieved, he sought to unify with the power in the Staff. An awareness of the Highest Wisdom flowed through him. His great love for God, as powerful as it was without the Staff, was currently amplified a thousand times. The Staff seemed to speak to him, questioning again and again whether the responsibility and actions that he now bore was for the sake of Heaven. For Afshin, blinded by his pride and prejudice answered it with an arrogant 'YES!' each time the thought entered him.

Afshin could never relate to others the prophetic experience if he had to. How could he explain a state where all opposites come together- love and hate, fear and brevity, physical and spiritual and a score of others surging like electricity throughout his entire being?

Ordering the command was child's play; he merely needed to envision what he wished to accomplish and the rest was up to the power within the Staff. Within minutes, the world's media all went to black. All methods of broadcast that previously apprised humanity of world events in a matter of seconds had all been disabled with one thought of Afshin's will.

He envisioned a resulting crescendo of fear. Initially, people would swear at the inconvenience of their cell phones getting cut off in the middle of their conversations. Upon redial, however, the lines wouldn't reconnect. At some point, they would falsely assume their carrier was experiencing an outage; nothing out of the ordinary. Soon after they would find their televisions, internet, landlines, and radios were no longer functional either; then the unease that something of far greater proportions would begin to creep into their minds. Perhaps another 9/11 attack? Or maybe the feared genius had finally managed to put his exceptional, twisted mind to maliciously implement the perfect electronic virus. Afshin meditated on the fact that the unknown would continue to proliferate as neighbors walked outside of homes and businesses to see if anything more was happening, only to find everyone else doing the same. Stepping outside would be the only way to determine if was anybody doing anything about whatever was happening. The neighborhoods would be simultaneously reassured and frightened by the loud blaring of the sirens as police cars drove by, going to various destinations in an attempt to manage the growing panicking crowds. The people had electricity, but little else. In an instant, communication was thrown back to pre-radio days of the early twentieth century. The masses could do nothing to gain an understanding of their situation but walk outside and talk with neighbors. Word-of-mouth communication was spreading worldwide, and Afshin delighted in the fact that life would soon return to the days of old, when things were simpler and infidels did not rule the world.

The growing rush of adrenaline was now ruling Afshin's motives. He wanted it all too fast. Rather than wait until he returned to the warehouse and meditate in his usual surroundings, he moved to bring about his desires right then. But just as he began imposing his will upon the world, the soft, muffled knocking of knuckles on the wooden door pulled him out of his meditation. Though the knocking was soft, for Afshin it was if bass drums had exploded during a symphonic moment. He stifled his anger and regained his composure in the short time that it took for him to hide the Staff and unlock the door.

The medical examiner was standing on the other side fixed on Afshin, who appeared to have either just awoken from sleep or was simply weary from his loss.

"I'm so sorry to disturb you," the man said in a mixed tone of sympathy and business, "but I've finished the initial work on your boss. Without opening the body to verify, it appears that Mohsen suffered a massive myocardial infarction. Quite unusual for a man as fit as he was. Especially without any prior symptoms. Had he been complaining about pains, dizziness or weakness at all, over the last few days?"

"No. Nothing," Afshin replied. "He was just making some sandwiches at our warehouse kitchen when he screamed in pain and collapsed."

"I see. Well, based on this information, we'll have to keep the body here for further testing. We ask the mourners to stay if possible, but you are welcome to go. I am assuming that you'll want to get some rest. Tomorrow will probably be a big day for you."

Afshin nodded his head in agreement, producing a closed-lipped smile. "Yes," he said, "tomorrow will indeed be a long day."

The medical examiner put his hand on Afshin's shoulder. "I understand. Would you like us to contact his relatives? It would be one less item that you'll have to attend to."

"No. No thank you. That won't be necessary. I'll go back to the office and wait until morning. Then, I will contact his children. Thank you for all your help."

The examiner flashed a sympathetic smile with a slight nod of the head. As he walked away Afshin remained alone in the entryway. He waited until the man had turned the corner and returned to retrieve the Staff. He looked one more time down the hall to verify nobody was around and hurried to the exit.

The frustration of coming so close to launching his plan only to have it pulled from under him in a wisp of a moment built up inside. Afshin couldn't wait to get out of the morgue and back to the warehouse. He once again moved about quickly and quietly out the main morgue entrance and to his black Mercedes that he had used to follow the ambulance.

Afshin started the car, yanked out of the parking lot and quickly turned onto the adjoining avenue en route back to the warehouse. Now that the moment was available Afshin struggled once again to calm himself, but the excitement again built into anxiety.

As he drove, a change of thought started to emerge. Of selfish nature, the thought originated from the evil impulse sadly prevalent in every man. The power he now possessed brought about the selfish thinking from which most men in similar positions suffer. He began to question why he should remain anonymous during a time when all life would change. After all, he reasoned, *he* controlled the power of the Staff. *He* could make things go the way he wanted while shielding himself from any harm. All the survivors of earth would then have to pay homage to *him*- the half-prophet who manipulated the powers of the Staff for the first time in three thousand years!

208 | Jeff Wedgle

Yes, he convinced himself in a short period of time, revealing himself to the world as God's chosen one is the way it should be.

His growing anxiousness became consuming. Afshin needed something to happen quickly, for everything was unfolding far too slowly for him to cope with. Then the thought came to him. *He* was the possessor of the Staff. Time should be under *his* control, not the other way around. Reactively, he pulled the car over to the side of the road.

At such an early time of the day, the car was as good as any place to manipulate the Staff. He turned off the vehicle, noticing how the outskirts of Tehran were so peaceful at this time of day. All was quiet as the sleeping city savored the last few minutes of predawn. Afshin soaked in the moment before reaching to the back seat to retrieve the treasured piece. The familiar feeling slowly enveloped him as the stone in the Staff came back to life, acknowledging Afshin was successfully entering the needed state of mind. With great care, he recalled his knowledge of ancient Hebrew and began the chant. The world media would now resume, but the first and only images will be of him. Right now. Live. Bringing to fruition, in a God's minute, the Eternal plan, he would become instantly become known as the Chosen One.

30

Glenn felt like he hadn't slept in months. In captivity, he had everything he wanted, but having so much time on his hands allowed his mind to be overrun with terrible anxiety. Even as he lied on the extremely elaborate and cozy bed furnished by Mohsen, he was no closer to sleep than he was on the airplane ride to Israel.

He wondered how Chayim was doing in the adjacent room. Glenn wanted to get up and knock on Chayim's door but he didn't want to risk waking his friend up. He turned on the light and grabbed the television remote that was still on the bed top from the last time he used it.

State-run Iranian television provided most of the programming choices and couldn't be more different than American television, dominated with news propaganda and religious themed channels. Additionally, the number of channels was quite limited.

Even with the luxuries of their condominium cage, the influence of the Iranian world outside through the TV set perpetuated the unease already festering inside him. *"One planet, but not one world,"* Glenn thought to himself.

With the TV on, Glenn did what he always did at home when sleep eluded him. He jumped out of bed and dropped to the floor to do pushups and sit-ups. Almost immediately he felt better. Not good enough to fall asleep, but at least his mind was occupied. In between sets of pushups he stopped and rested to watch a news channel broadcast. Glenn wished he could understand what the newscaster was saying. He also just wanted to know what was *really* going on in the outside world.

He muted the volume with the remote since he couldn't understand anyway and chuckled to himself why he hadn't thought of that earlier. He turned around on the floor for another set of pushups. The second set was harder than the first. He could only manage ten this time. He sat up to rest. At first he paid no attention to the images from the television, but as he looked closer he saw that, while the newscaster was talking, a picture of their captor, Mohsen, was on the backdrop. Glenn instinctively turned up the sound, which of course frustrated him when he heard Persian coming from the newscaster's mouth. Helpless to understand what was being said, Glenn just sat and watched, hoping that a visual cue might help him figure out why they were talking about Mohsen on TV. He didn't have to wait long before he found out why. The next images showed some on-the-scene footage of an ambulance with a stretcher being pushed into it. On the stretcher was a body covered head to toe by a white cloth. After the footage had completed, the newscaster re-appeared with Mohsen's picture superimposed again on the screen. This time they had the dates 1948-2012 inscribed below it. Glenn had troubles trying to convince himself that Mohsen was dead.

He picked himself up off the floor and cracked open the door of his room to see if any 'babysitters' were watching. Surprisingly, the main room was quiet and empty. He snuck down the hall and over to Chayim's room and swung the door open. To Glenn's surprise, Chayim wasn't in bed, rather, he stood facing the wall-to-ceiling windows that overlooked Tehran. Chayim was praying in the usual back and forth motion typical of Jewish worshippers. Hearing the door open, Chayim jumped at the thought of who was entering. Anticipating the worst to happen he assumed the unexpected entry into his room was a signal of impending doom. He relaxed a little when he saw that it was only Glenn.

"Can you knock first next time?" a frustrated Chayim asked. "You're going to give me heart failure!"

"Do you think it would've really helped?" asked Glenn. "You'd have jumped a mile high even if I did knock. Listen, I had the TV on. I was watching the news. They flashed a picture of Mohsen. I think he's dead!"

"Wha... wh?" Chayim stuttered trying to register the information.

212 | Jeff Wedgle

"There was a picture of Mohsen on the news, but I couldn't understand what the newscaster was saying. But then I saw some footage of a body being taken away in an ambulance. Then, they flipped back to the newscaster and showed Mohsen's picture again, this time with dates. You know, how they usually put dates up to show that an important person died? Jesus, I can't believe it! What now?" Glenn seemed to be searching the room for answers, even though his question was rhetorical.

"Are you *sure* that it was Mohsen?" asked Chayim finally digesting the information.

"Positive! Besides, none of his goons are in the main room right now. I think in all the chaos, they up and left. They probably thought we'd never figure out we're alone. Even if we did, what could we possibly do about it? Run to the nearest police station? We really are marooned in the middle of civilization!"

Chayim was wondering how they might capitalize on the opportunity. "Let's look and see if anybody is in the hallway now."

The two quietly looked in all the rooms of the condo to be sure that there was no one in site. Indeed, they were alone. They walked to the front door leading from the condo to the main hallway. Glenn quietly peeked through the peephole in the door. What limited sight was available to him showed no one standing immediately near the door. "Nobody's out there," he whispered to Chayim.

The two returned to the living room and looked out the window to the world that lay a hundred feet below them. Darkness blanketed the early morning on the streets. Glenn and Chayim sat down on the living room chairs to determine their next moves. It was difficult for them to determine where to begin. They had been smuggled into Iran by Mohsen, who was now dead. As captives in a high-rise condominium somewhere in Tehran, a completely foreign city, they found themselves with no money, no transportation, no friends, and nowhere to go.

"We need to get out of here before someone decides we shouldn't have been left alone," Glenn whispered emphatically trying to keep the urgency from turning to panic.

"Agreed," replied Chayim, "but where will we go? We have no money, and we'll stick out like sore thumbs the minute we hit the streets. Especially me- look at me! They'll shoot me dead before I get to the end of the block!"

"Not necessarily. Have you checked the closet in your room by chance?"

"No."

"Neither have I... yet. First off, let's see if there's anything we can change into so we won't look so obvious. From there we can look around for maps or money or anything that we might be able to use."

Both of them rose up and went off to their respective rooms to peruse the closets. Glenn's room was the master and had a reasonably well-stocked closet with an eclectic collection of clothing. If this were Mohsen's place, he apparently had different sets of clothes for every occasion. Glenn found a black suit, a

214 | Jeff Wedgle

brown suit, some pants and some casual shirts. He also found a long, white, robe-like tunic- typical garb for a religious Muslim which he had seen on the streets in America. He never did learn the name of those things. As he looked at the tunic, he imagined Chayim would look more natural in it. In fact, if Chayim wore the tunic then Glenn, with his fair skin, would simply appear as a guest of his.

"Yo, Chayim, did you find anything? I did."

"Nothing here. This looks like a guest room. The closet's practically empty. What did you find?"

"A tunic."

Chayim walked into the room. Glenn had left the television on. "You'll look ridiculous in that without a beard and head covering," he mused.

"Ah, but this is for you my friend," Glenn replied with a smile.

"Surely you're kidding."

"Look Chayim," Glenn said with unwavering seriousness. "We don't have much time, if any. You've got a beard and the look of a religious man. It makes sense for you to wear this!"

"But you've got to know how this feels. I'm an orthodox Jew, and I'm going to wear the garb of a devout Muslim?" Chayim realized his rationalization was flawed.

"You yourself said I'd stand out if I wore it," Glenn said making his point. "If we have a chance to make it out of here, we cannot risk drawing any unwanted attention to ourselves and you know it."

Chayim said nothing. He knew Glenn was right. He sighed deeply and took the tunic from Glenn and slipped it on over his head. Once the tunic and the headcover were on him, Chayim easily passed as a Muslim. Glenn smiled nodding his head in an emphatic endorsement.

"Okay," Glenn continued to orchestrate. "At least now you look like someone from the streets, and I'm a visitor. Not as conspicuous as *both* of us appearing that way. Hopefully this will keep suspicion down, at least long enough for us to figure out where we're going next."

Chayim looked around the apartment. "Let's see if there's anything in here that we could use."

The two began their search. Glenn went into the kitchen while Chayim went into the second bedroom where he was staying. He recalled seeing a pile of paperwork earlier on top of the desk in there. Chayim hoped the papers might reveal something that might help them.

Meanwhile, Glenn turned the light on in the kitchen. It was small and neatly kept, stocked with the usual kitchen gadgets and utensils. A small table for two stood in the corner. Glenn looked around for anything of use. A small magnetic key ring on the side of the refrigerator caught his eye. He went to examine the keys. The key ring held several keys that appeared to be shaped for doors of an office building or home, probably for the building they were in. To be sure, he took the ring and tried several on the front door of the apartment. After several attempts, the seventh key proved to be a match. Also on the ring were two car keys, easily identified by the fancy Mercedes Benz logo on the rubber handle. Closer examination showed they were not duplicates of one another, which probably meant they were for two different cars altogether. Chayim entered the room a few moments later.

"I found some papers that happened to have some English on them," he informed Glenn. "It seems that Mohsen is... er, was a big shot in antiquities. I found a letter written in English. It goes on to disclose a delivery at his warehouse, and gives the address. Glenn, if he's stashing other antiques there, I think there's a pretty good chance the Staff could be there as well."

"Possibly. Okay, so what if it is? How will we find the location of the warehouse? How do we get there? How will we get in? And even if we do, then what? We're not going to be able to just skate out of this country Chayim!" Glenn fought the feelings of panic that once again started to emerge in both of them.

"I don't know those answers," Chayim replied stoically. But I do know that we're here because of Divine will. Remember Glenn, *we* found the Staff. We're involved... and I know that God is too. Let those questions be His to answer. In the meantime, I think the first order of business is to get to the Staff based on what we know. We have the address, now all we need is to figure out where the warehouse is, and how to get there."

"These may help," Glenn said with a bit more ease. He was twirling the set of car keys around his finger. "Mercedes. A high rise building like this has to have a parking facility. Let's get down there and see what kind of luck we have."

"Great, but even if we find the car, then what? Everything is written in Persian. We can't just go around looking for a building that says 'Mohsen's Building'," Chayim asked somewhat rhetorically.

"We need a map, or better yet, a computer. Was there anything else in that room?"

"There's a desk. I found the papers on the top, but there are also two drawers to it that are locked."

"Well, I just may be able to remedy that," Glenn replied hopefully reaching for the key ring. "These may be for the desk or even the warehouse, if we ever find it."

They both hurried to the second room and the desk that sat facing the large window. Glenn was happy to see that it was still pitch dark outside. The hostile world that awaited them was still asleep. He took the smaller set of keys and tried each, one by one. Soon, he found one that fit inside the lock. With increased hope, Glenn turned the key and opened the drawer to discover more papers. Glenn took them out and ordered Chayim, "Here, look through these and see if there's anything useful. I'll see if I can find a-" Glenn stopped in mid sentence as he opened the second drawer. "Never mind," he said practically singing. "Look what I found!" He held up a laptop computer and wasted no time in turning it on. "Please God, don't let there be a password on this thing." But as the words left his lips, the splash screen soon appeared with the usual 'Please enter your name and password' text boxes. "Shit! Come on God! Would you please make this a little easier on us?" Glenn tried the only thing he knew. He found Mohsen's name on one of the papers and typed it in for both the user name and password. The computer accepted them and continued toward the desktop. "Thanks God," he said.

The computer was slow to boot up. Once at the desktop, Glenn immediately launched the internet application but it failed to show any websites.

"Is the wireless button on?" Glenn asked himself hurriedly. The button was on but was not making contact with a wireless network. "Looks like he doesn't have internet here. We need to find a place that does. Okay, let's get downstairs. Either we find a car or I don't know what. But I'm not coming back up here. Who knows when Mohsen's henchmen will be back for us? Our survival is as far away from this place as possible!"

The two gathered up the computer and headed quietly for the apartment door. Chayim cautiously opened it and scouted the hallway. It was still empty. The boys walked down the hall to a small elevator. For a luxury apartment building, the elevator was in poor condition and doubtfully could accommodate more than four people. Chayim looked at the buttons and pressed one marked by Persian lettering. It was the lowest positioned button and Chayim assumed it was the parking level. The elevator slowly worked its way down and, what seemed to take forever, stopped at the desired level. To their relief they had arrived in the parking garage which appeared to contain roughly eighty cars or so. The duo walked out of the elevator and combed through the lanes for a vehicle that bore the Mercedes insignia. As they walked, Glenn, holding the keys, remembered that the Mercedes key had an 'unlock' button and pressed it. A shiny, black car in the first parking spot flashed its lights.

"Jeez, first parking spot. Mohsen must have been a real special guy," Glenn said in elated sarcasm.

"Influential too. He'd have to be for his death to make the news," continued Chayim.

Chayim took the keys from Glenn to execute the charade, should anyone see them. Taking no chances, they both agreed that Glenn would take the backseat in case he had to hide. Thankfully, the windows were tinted black to further disguise the two. Chayim started the car and backed out of the space. He slowly drove forward, past the parked cars to the exit just fifty yards ahead.

He drew in a long breath to try and calm down. The prospect of driving around the streets of Tehran was nerve-racking. He felt like his chest was going to explode.

The car steadily rolled up the basement ramp and onto the immediate side street. Mundane driving mechanics were now at the conscious level: what side of the street to drive on; or what stop signs look like. They simply could not afford to attract attention while driving. Chayim drove like a white-head, the term he used to call old people at home. He drove straight down the middle of the street, which was lined with apartment homes. The streets were clean and adorned with palm trees. Chayim noticed none of it as he gripped the steering wheel for dear life. His knuckles were white and his mouth was as dry as the desert. He broke into a sweat as his breathing became labored.

"I can't do this Glenn," Chayim said as he panicked. "I'm going to faint!"

"Take it easy buddy," Glenn said calmly. But he too felt panic. "Remember what you told me about God taking you on this journey? It's true! We're here because He wants us to be here." Glenn's earnest reply was beginning to diffuse the tension.

"Okay, okay. You're right, I still believe it. As it says in the book of Joshua, 'Be strong and of strong spirit.' It's true. I'm okay. Where are we going?" Though it didn't sound assuring, Chayim was actually gaining a hold on the panic.

"Let's try and look for a commercial district of some sort and pray that we find a place where we can get an internet signal."

The two drove slowly around the lit streets of the city still in a residential neighborhood. Cars were parked erratically in front of apartments, not much different than in Israeli cities. Chayim stopped at every intersection afraid he overlooked a stop sign. At one point, a car nearly rear ended them when Chayim stopped at an intersection he shouldn't have. The other driver screeched to a halt and wailed on his horn for a good ten seconds. Apparently, there was little forgiveness for night drivers.

After much time was spent navigating through residential areas, a section of town came into view that appeared to be a small commercial area. It too was clean, but very old and very charming. As Chayim relaxed somewhat, he thought Iran would be a great place to visit if it weren't for the lunatics running the country. They drove down a small hill which had a traffic light at the bottom to a main thoroughfare. Chayim stopped at the light and looked both ways up and down the intersecting street. The area seemed to be a little artsy section with all the shops featuring pottery, paintings, sculptures and various supplies in their windows. Everything was closed as far as Chayim could see. When the light changed, Chayim made a right hand turn onto the thoroughfare.

"I'll look on the right and you look on the left," said Chayim.

Store after store rolled by. Some had gates in front of their windows. Others had special green-colored paint on their doors. Glenn remembered this was an Islamic tradition known to keep away bad spirits.

Suddenly, Glenn shouted from the back seat. "Look over there! On the left! Look what it says in the window!" Sure enough, among the myriad of other writings on its window, a store with its lights on boasted the words 'Wi-Fi'. It was a quaint coffee shop of which only a few patrons were seated at the sparse tables inside. One side of the store was adjacent to an alleyway and Chayim needed no instruction. He turned into the alley and turned down the lights of the car, but left the engine running. Glenn, in his desire to save computer battery, had turned the laptop off earlier. Rebooting it seemed to take a lifetime. After punching in Mohsen's username and password, he connected to the network and launched a browser window. Within a few but seemingly long seconds, the default internet page came on and Glenn shouted a quiet 'Yes!' from the back seat. He brought up 'Google Maps' and entered the address of Mohsen's warehouse they had found from the stacks of papers in Chayim's room. Glenn had stuck the paper in his pocket. He clicked on 'satellite view' and the address yielded an image of the warehouse and surrounding area. Glenn zoomed in to show a more detailed street map. He lifted the laptop higher so that Chayim could look as well. The two studied it as they tried to recognize anything familiar in it.

"I recognize this spot here!" Chayim exclaimed pointing to the screen. "See that thing there? We passed something like it about ten minutes ago. If that's it, we passed by Mohsen's warehouse!" The structure was taller than any of the buildings around it. It appeared to be an old water tower that supplied water to the city before the area had plumbing and sewage. It was in very close proximity to Mohsen's warehouse. "Let's head back that way. We've been here too long and need to move on before the store owner gets suspicious."

Chayim put the car in reverse and backed out of the alley to return to the direction from which they came.

*   *   *

Though the streets seemed to offer some visual cues to Chayim, navigating on instinct alone produced little progress. Their search continued for nearly half an hour. Every turn of the car began with new hope and ended in disappointment. Eventually, they came upon a street that overlooked a large hill with industrial looking warehouses scattered along it. Not far from them was the large water tower. They had meandered so far away from their original location they now viewed the structure from a completely different angle than from when Chayim first noticed it. Somehow, they needed to traverse to the other side of the hill, through another set of residential high rises and commercial center. Gradually they wove their way across through dimly lit streets and dead-ends, eventually finding their way to the base of the water tower. It looked exactly like the one on the map.

"From here, we go three blocks to the east and take a left," Glenn instructed from the back seat. "Do you know which way is east?" he asked.

"I'm seeing a bit of day cresting on the horizon. I think it's this way." Chayim pointed to his left.

He found a block that would take them east and proceeded down to an area filled by large warehouses.

"What's the number of Mohsen's place?" Chayim asked.

"Glenn looked at the number that was on the paper. The number was 232. Since they couldn't read the signs, the name of the street was meaningless. Chayim drove cautiously down the street. To their amazement, on their right was a medium-sized building that contained a door on the front side. Above the door, the numbers 232 were lit up by the building's entryway lights.

31

"I love technology!" said Glenn triumphantly.

"It is pretty amazing that we found it," Chayim replied, nearly as enthusiastic.

Before the two could become complacent in their success, the next challenge immediately faced them. They now had to find a way into the warehouse, and that presented a new host of potential obstacles; how would they gain access? Was there a burglar alarm, or perhaps guard dogs? Were Mohsen's men waiting to ambush them from the inside? As these questions raced through their minds, they harkened back to what Glenn said earlier about being chosen. They had been chosen as part of a Divine decree and this was enough to give them the strength needed to overcome their fears.

From what little they could see, no one appeared to be in or around the warehouse. This was sort of expected though, as the local time appeared to be no later than six a.m. But to be sure, Chayim turned off the main road and parked the car on the side of the building behind two commercially sized trash bins.

"I think this is where Mohsen died," Glenn informed Chayim. "I recognize from the news footage the front door where they took the body out. It's surprising to me that no one would be here. You know, like those yellow-taped crime scenes on TV?"

"Where do you think you're at? Downtown Manhattan?" Chayim asked sarcastically? "He probably died late yesterday or into last night. Or at least that's when he was found. His henchmen then probably left with the body to the morgue. Think about the apartment we were in- they left us *completely* alone. They're probably so preoccupied trying to figure out what to do after his death. And *that's* why I think time is of the essence! I'll bet they'll be on their way back to the apartment or here before long. So let's try those keys on the door."

Glenn and Chayim got out of the car, double-checking to see if anyone was in the immediate vicinity. Since they were in an industrial area, they didn't expect anyone else to be around yet, and fortunately that proved to be the case. The lighting over the front door made it easy for them to examine the door lock and keys. Glenn wasted no time testing each key, in every possible direction. Some of the keys actually fit into the lock but weren't able to turn it. Growing frustrated, he tried to force one of the keys that fit, jiggling and bending the key, but it simply refused to comply. With hope and desperation, Glenn tried each key once again, but the same results met them the second time. Deflated, they realized getting into the warehouse would be more difficult than they had hoped.

Glenn searched for an alternate entry. He looked for windows and other doors into the building. The only windows were at the top of the warehouse which appeared to be as tall as three stories. Next to one of the windows was a drain pipe leading from the roof to the ground. The only thing Glenn could think to do was to climb up the pipe and break in through the window, hoping to find a way down on the other side.

"Those windows seem to be our only way of getting in," Glenn said. "I'll climb up the pipe and shatter that first window. Let's just hope we don't attract any attention when I do."

Chayim was more than willing to let Glenn climb the pipe. This was one of the few times he was glad he wasn't as athletic as Glenn. Several tall, wide branched Cyprus trees were adjacent to the pipe, easily within reach of it. Glenn figured he could climb the trees first and only when he couldn't get any closer to the windows, he could grab the pipe and climb it the rest of the way up.

"I'm going to start climbing. Why don't you go around the building again, just to make sure that this is the easiest way in."

Glenn took a long, deep breath to calm his nerves, and began the ascent up the cypress. He was already a third of the way up by the time Chayim left to find an alternative way in. The higher he went up, the further he was away from the door's night lights. The darkness made it difficult to find his footing.

He was nearly half way to the window when the tree swayed slightly in the night breeze. Glenn's legs quivered. His thigh muscles burned maintaining his balance, as he released his hands from one branch to secure another. The effort near the top was tedious as the branches were getting thinner and the tree swayed more. Glenn fought back the fear that he might inadvertently step onto a branch that couldn't support him, sending him plummeting to the ground. He could see the window and the vague outline of the pipe against the darkened wall. From this angle Glenn could also see that the windows were inset from the edge of the building. The ledge appeared to be large enough that he could sit on it. *Eight more feet to go.* The cypress swayed a little more. The ground looked like it was hundreds of feet down, even though it was probably a little over twenty-five. Glenn felt a drop of perspiration from his forehead roll down over his face, tickling as it went. He prayed it would keep from his eyes as he dare not let go of the branch, even for a moment, to wipe it away.

From his position on the tree, the window ledge was just out of reach without the further assistance of the drain pipe. Glenn reached out to the pipe, jiggling it to check its stability. There was only a slight give to it which gave minimal assurance that the pipe was strong enough to support him. He hugged the drain with both hands and pushed off from the tree with his legs. In a swift motion, his legs wrapped around the pipe and he was now three feet from the base of the window.

The final push to the top reminded Glenn of his workout back at the gym he belonged to which was equipped with ropes and climbing walls. He inched up the drain like a monkey on a vine, up to the base of the window ledge. The transition from the pipe to the ledge at this height was daunting. Unlike the gym at home, there was no net to break his fall. He raised one leg onto the ledge. Having the strain removed from the other, his hands bore the brunt of his body weight, giving his aching thighs a rest. After pausing a few moments to catch his breath, he brought his other leg onto the ledge. Once in position, he pushed his hands from the pipe and clamped them on the ledge to keep from tumbling to the ground. Once he felt stable enough, Glenn laid on his back, his whole body using every inch of the ledge as he tried to release the tension from his quadriceps, biceps and shoulders.

Once he gathered himself, he carefully turned his body around to face the window. He held onto the sides of the windowsill as he carefully looked down to the interior of the warehouse. Wondering of his whereabouts, Glenn looked down away from the window, searching for Chayim. As he was looking down, the window next to him suddenly snapped open. Glenn jerked back, startled from the sound and felt his grip slip from the sides of the sill. Instinctively, Glenn reached his hand out onto the side of the pane that had swung open, enabling him to regain his center of gravity back onto the ledge and saving him from the backward three-story plunge. Just then, Chayim's smiling face peered out of the window from the inside of the warehouse.

"You son of a bitch!" Glenn screamed, ignoring their desire to remain hidden. "You almost fucking killed me!" Glenn was wide-eyed and breathing heavy. He felt like slugging Chayim if only he was in the position to do so.

"Shh!" Chayim hushed him, extending his hand out for Glenn to grab onto. Glenn took it and clumsily fell into the other side of the window onto the old metal catwalk that enabled access from the inside of the building to the high windows. The cumulative effect of the climbing, stress and close encounter with death had Glenn straining for his breath. Several minutes later, his breathing started to become normal again.

"Sorry about that," Chayim said quietly. "I guess I should have lightly knocked on the window first. I went behind the building and climbed the fence to the side of the building we couldn't see the first time. I found a small window to the toilet and it was propped open, most likely by the last user for obvious reasons. I came around to the front to tell you, but you were already too high up and I didn't want to shout so I figured I'd climb in there and at least open the window for you. But by the time I got here, you were already on the ledge. I'm sorry I scared you."

"Jesus, Chayim," Glenn answered, "you opened that window like you were trying to escape from a fire!"

Glenn avoided any more conversation. He now had the chance to wipe the perspiration from his head and eyes and regain his calm. "So what have you seen in here so far?"

"All the stuff that Mohsen imported. Crates from all over the world stacked two and three high. He must do some big business. His warehouse looks like the ending from *Raiders of the Lost Ark*."

"Anything specific?"

"Don't know. I really was just trying to get up here to let you in."

"Alright... I'm ready," breathed Glenn after a brief moment. The adrenaline had finally stopped pumping. "Let's go see what we can find."

32

Afshin was still on the side of the road when he slowly came back from the Other World. Once alert, he found that somehow he was live over the airwaves. His image adorned every television and computer screen, his voice over every speaker, whether over the radio, computer or television. Energized by the new power he possessed, he started the car and resumed his drive back to the warehouse. He introduced himself only as 'the One' and engaged in the stereotypical soap box lecture of man's sinfulness.

The initial impact of these images left viewers, which included the World's top political and military leaders, puzzled. First assumptions indicated a coup in a rogue state, since Afshin was virtually unknown. He then gave forth another clue to his identity and next introduced himself as an Iranian National who had been, and always would be, loyal to the Ayatollahs, from Khomeini onward. But then he explained his total frustration of the slow, deliberate pace in which those same leaders were ushering in the destruction of the West. The World sat paralyzed as they were forced to listen to the judgment of their executioner.

"Your governments have led you astray. Many opportunities have been afforded to you to embrace the one, true religion! Yet, you have shunned away from the truth. You have sinned! You have promoted immorality! You have embraced the false god of currency. The Crusaders of Christ are guilty for your centuries of persecution and spilled blood. You have created a state of murderers in our midst- the Zionists! Pathetic Palestinian leaders have sinned by even considering making peace with those despicable Jews and their gutter-based religion! Even those fighting in Gaza- the mere fact you agreed to a cease-fire, are guilty of running away from the responsibility of your Jihad! You are weak, you are guilty, and you have been judged by God, Who has dispatched me to carry out your sentence!"

Afshin lectured on and on as he drove to the warehouse. The planet was handcuffed and paralyzed, forced to listen to the views of one man's propaganda who was fed lies as an impressionable adolescent. He had learned the 'truth' from the leaders, they were so honest and caring.

All military systems were disabled- from the ignitions of jets and helicopters to the codes that launched warheads; even the ability to track the very location of a madman who had full control of all media.

Fifteen minutes of nonstop admonition later Afshin was at the warehouse. Two cars were parked in front of the warehouse. One belonged to Pamesh, one of Mohsen's bodyguards. Strangely, so was Mohsen's other black Mercedes from the apartment building. Then it donned on Afshin that their American Jewish friends had paid them a visit.

Upon seeing Afshin's car pull up, the bodyguard immediately sprang from his car and rushed to Afshin's to open the door for him.

"I couldn't sleep since we took Mohsen to the morgue," Pamesh said hurriedly as though he had just one moment to speak to a king. "So I was up when you suddenly were on the television. I heard what you said. It was sensational! So I drove here. I will be your faithful servant!"

Afshin smiled at Pamesh as he opened the back door of the car to retrieve the Staff. Upon seeing the ancient artifact and its mild glow of bluish-green, the bodyguard immediately fell to his knees.

"You are truly the anointed one! You have been given the gift of communication with The Divine!" The man would not even raise his head in fear of punishment for such a disrespectful act.

"Get up Pamesh," Afshin ordered the bowing man. "Your dedication to God and your faith have impressed me. You will stand by me as we do God's Will. Besides, we have some guests inside. I think you'll find amusing their surprise when they see us."

Afshin unlocked the front door of the warehouse and the two men proceeded to go inside.

33

Inside the warehouse was just as Chayim had described. The main floor hosted thousands of square feet with crates from places such as Singapore, the Philippines and Hong Kong. Some crates were marked describing their contents such as china, textiles, even toilet seats. Surprisingly, the wording was written in English. Glenn and Chayim walked along a row of storage looking vainly for a clue to lead them to the whereabouts of the Staff.

"It's gonna take *forever* to go through these boxes," Glenn remarked in frustration.

Chayim replied, "I don't think Mohsen would have the Staff boxed up. Remember what he said? He wanted to use it to become the greatest Muslim that ever lived. If anything, I think he would have it in some special place, or even in his possession. I think we need to investigate the offices. He wasn't done with the Staff and was probably still trying to figure out how to use it to execute his jacked-up plan before he died."

Glenn nodded in agreement and the two made their way to some offices upstairs.

The back side of the warehouse contained a metal staircase that led to a second level. Chayim motioned to the rooms at the top. The morning sun began to lighten up the windows as they cautiously ascended the metal staircase.

The second floor was elaborately decorated. Artifacts of every variety adorned the walls and bookcases. The beauty of the second floor implied Mohsen spent a lot of time there. He had surrounded himself with the finest of what the world's countries and history could offer. A small kitchenette was off to the left while two more rooms with closed doors were down the hall to the right. A small room with a glass door sat opposite the kitchenette. It appeared to be a humidor.

"Mohsen probably had this room built to look at old documents," Glenn said as they looked in through the room's clear glass door. They passed up that room and elected to first inspect the rooms down the hall, figuring the last one was Mohsen's door. The first door they came to was unlocked so they opened it, turned on the light and peeked inside. It was a windowless, carpeted room with two yoga mats lying on the ground. The mats were separated by a small, contemporary wooden coffee table. This room also reminded Glenn of his gym in New York with the meditative quality of this windowless space. It was quite similar to the atmosphere of the gym's Tai Chi room. With the exception of the mats, table, and table accessories, the room was empty. Glenn figured this was where Mohsen went to relax during working hours and thus, was the reason for the sparse amount of furniture and fixtures. On the table was adorned with an unlit candle and a cloth. The overhead lights provided little luminosity.

The duo walked into the room. Chayim proceeded over to the table to examine the candle and cloth. Glenn followed quickly after him. Closer examination revealed the cloth was in fact the shroud that enclosed The Holy Staff.

"It's the shroud to the Staff!" exclaimed Chayim excitedly.

He pondered his surroundings. This room was set up for meditation. Perhaps, it donned on him, *this* was where Mohsen was training to use the Staff. Chayim learned at his school in Israel that meditation was essential for one to achieve a prophetic state. This room now made sense to him.

He looked at Glenn who was holding the shroud, feeling its fabric. Even here in the sanctuary of a megalomaniac it still brought reverence. "Mohsen used this room to meditate to try and use the Staff," he said.

"Meditate?"

"Yeah- in order to achieve the level of consciousness necessary to employ the Staff. He had to work on his mindset in order to use it."

"I see," Glenn reflected. "So he made this room up for his 'needs'. Makes sense. But why are there *two* mats? He must have been training with someone."

"That *someone* was his teacher, though Mohsen would never have admitted that," came a voice from the room's entrance. Glenn and Chayim spun around to see a slight man at the door. He was holding the Staff. Next to him was another man holding and running a sophisticated camera.

The undersized man continued, "I presume you've come for *this*." He held the holy artifact for the two to see it.

The boys didn't know who Afshin was and Afshin was in no hurry to give them any details. "Yes gentlemen. *I* am the teacher. Mohsen was, and always will be just a student."

"Who are you?" Chayim challenged, anticipating the worst.

"That is none of your concern," Afshin replied forcefully. "And take off those clothes! They are reserved for the holy lions!" The man spoke like a true zealot. He told Chayim to remove the frock that they found in Mohsen's closet, barely concealing his racism. Chayim quickly took it off along with the head covering.

"Mohsen had you brought here for assistance with the Staff, but my knowledge is much greater, and my training successful. That is why *I* possess the Staff. You will bear witness to why *I* am the teacher. The power of the Staff flows again because of *me*, and my love and devotion to *my* faith! Allah the Great, Master of All, has personally chosen *me* to fulfill the world's purpose!"

The man spoke like any religious radical on TV. The difference was, this fanatic had the Staff in his hand. Glenn wondered if this clown was responsible for Mohsen's death. He couldn't tell from the newscast how Mohsen had died, but he certainly could have been murdered by the lunatic standing in front of them. Glenn fished for information.

"You're the reason Mohsen is dead aren't you?"

"Mohsen was chosen by God the Great to bring the Staff to me. After that, his mission was complete and he could no longer serve God's purpose on earth." Afshin continued to avoid direct answers. "But now, in the name of Allah, is the beginning of God's redemption to His people!" The man's eyes were wide with conviction, his piercing gaze seemed to allude to the future. His patience grew thin with the few questions that had been asked of him. "There is no need to talk anymore! You and the world will bear witness to the great chaos that awaits to commence the eternal, new world order."

34

Afshin wasted no time setting into motion his plan to punish the infidels. The long list of sinners began with Israel, the United Kingdom and America. Alongside them would be Cairo and Istanbul. It was the price to be paid for their secularity.

The wait had been so long and painful, but today, the agony would cease... *forever*. With the Staff, all of this would come about in minutes with no earthly repercussions; a gift from the Almighty. The world was his.

Afshin instructed Pamesh to tie up Glenn and Chayim and immobilize them in the corner of the room. He then assumed the meditative position on the yoga mat, keeping the Staff in his possession all the while. Complete silence oppressed the room. Glenn and Chayim dared not utter a word, fearing they would be killed instantly if they did so. They stood by, helpless to alter the course of events that would surely follow; they had no choice but to watch.

The two observed in horror as Afshin sat down on the mat and worked into meditative consciousness. Some time passed before the sapphire stone in the Staff began to glow, much brighter than before. Something was definitely happening. Seconds later, appearing from nowhere, the room's walls became littered with large plasma television monitors. Real-time images of Israeli, English and American cities filled the screens. Scenes from Cairo joined the rest. The scenes told the story; faces of anguish and despair. These faces had already witnessed the seizure of their media and their military and knew that the megalomaniac behind all of it was not simply making idle threats. He meant what he said. Glenn and Chayim now joined in the horror of what Afshin had set into motion.

All people of good will began to wonder if God had given up on mankind: most did not blame Him; but some still managed to curse at Him; while others knew this was not His bidding. Nevertheless, they all would be forced to watch their fate meted out over the airwaves. Their defenses stymied, they were helpless to do anything but pray and wait. Humankind would surely stay tuned to their radios, televisions and computers hopelessly watching as the live destruction played out on every media device in the world. Afshin delighted at the thought.

Rather than making them simply vanish, Afshin chose to use technology to destroy cities such as New York City, Washington, Istanbul, London and all of

Israel, including the Arab territories. How he would relish the burning and suffering of the sinful nations. The flying warheads, terrified faces of sinners, their helplessness illustrated on television screens, the impact of warheads on cities, burning, shockwaves, and all out chaos were what he wanted the world to remember forever.

Glenn and Chayim were pinned in the back of the room wishing this was all just a staged show; an electronic action game that they used to play as kids. The world they once knew was disappearing before their eyes, innocence eradicated by the tragic sickness of mankind; extremism.

The young men could not move. They could barely breathe. Tears rolled down their faces, knowing their attempts to seize the Staff had failed. They were helpless now; so very close to accomplishing, but thousands of miles from succeeding.

Pictures of Amman, Tel-Aviv, New York, Cairo, London, Washington and Jerusalem flashed across the giant monitors invisibly mounted all around the room. There was nowhere one could look to divert the gaze from what was unfolding.

Afshin had supported his government's past threats of wiping Israel off the map. Now, however, it would be he, not them, who would make that happen since they could not do it fast enough.

Afshin used the power of the Staff to seal all nuclear bomb shelters. Some images on the monitors showed the mass hysteria of people desperately trying to get the shelters open. Taunting laughter spewing from Pamesh's mouth seeped into the room as the television displayed young children clinging onto their desperate mothers who were trying vainly to open the shelter doors with kitchen knives.

Other monitors showed the Arab populations of Gaza and East Jerusalem running for cover. Though brothers, they too were condemned and it pained him to know that they also would certainly perish, but only from this world. Once the pain of dying was over, they would repent from their sin of negotiating with the Zionists and be accepted as martyrs forever in the next world. He smiled, imagining that all his Muslim brothers would soon regard him as the savior of modern times, the liberator of his people from the evils of the infidels.

The monitors continued to show the mayhem as Chayim cried as he helplessly watched the nightmare. Prayer was the only thing that remained within his power. He prayed, and when Glenn saw Chayim, he prayed along with him. As they prayed, they begged before The Only One, asking to stop the events that were taking place. But even as he prayed, Glenn questioned God, wondering if man's evils had taken them to a point where God no longer cared. Glenn was angry. One madman couldn't win and bring about the destruction of half the world. But in his soul, he knew that one madman certainly could. Glenn cursed Heavenward. Chayim was not as brazen. Even now, witnessing the unthinkable, he could never curse towards Heaven. He merely prayed and continued to repeat the main principle of his faith, 'The Lord is God, The Lord is One'.

Moments later, half of the room's monitors switched to aerial views of warheads leaving their earthly homes toward the sky. It seemed all the accusations that the government was placing warheads in residential neighborhoods were, in fact, true.

The nuclear warheads were on their way to their destinations. Tel-Aviv and Jerusalem were the first targets, as they were in closer proximity than The United States and England. The traitors that lived in the cities of Amman, Istanbul and Cairo were next. These cities had sinned; anything less than complete observance of The Holy Koran was blasphemy; there was no compromise otherwise.

Once the warheads had been fired, Afshin slowly emerged out of his trance. Fully conscious, he contently looked back and forth between the different monitors. They displayed all that he had commanded. A smile of satisfaction emerged on his face. He observed rockets headed straight for Tel-Aviv on one television, as another showed pandemonium ensuing in the city's streets. It would all be over soon enough and the impact would be catastrophic. People hurried into cars and boats, any means of transportation available, trying to outrun the inevitable, but there were too many trying to do the same causing gridlock everywhere. The streets were jammed with people, motor vehicles and pandemonium.

Much to Afshin's amusement, some of the monitors showed the infidels praying. Scenes from the

Old City of Jerusalem zeroed in on the Muslim Al-Aqsa Mosque and the Jewish Western Wall just below. Live depictions of worshipers, thousands of them, smashed together as closely as they could possibly be praying with all their might.

"Do they really think God is listening to them?" Afshin asked rhetorically to Pamesh.

Other monitors displayed something rather unexpected. Though people were engaged in prayer, there were even larger numbers crowding into the streets and they were not bent in prayer. Rather, they were marching by the thousands, punching their fists in the air while screaming, voicing their hatred toward Afshin for judging them; for judging them falsely. Thousands screamed in a frenzied chant, 'Death to the false messiah!' The residents of East Jerusalem hated Israel, but now it seemed the real enemy was their fellow Muslim, Afshin. At first, Afshin was shocked at the sight, but then it began to make sense to him- the Palestinians were cowards. They had lost their backbone when they chose to give up their Jihad in search of peace, or at least in their agreement to cease-fires. The resistance, on the contrary, should have been relentless and ongoing. Forget about the military capability of the enemy, these invertebrates would be defeated by God Himself. So, together, he comforted in the thought, the criminals and the cowards alike will join together in death, and the land will once again flourish with the faithful!

Less than a minute remained before the warheads were at the halfway point. Nothing could stop them now. Just over three minutes remained until the initial impact in Israel. For the victims, that was hardly time enough to say goodbye to their families and express their love to one another. For Afshin, however, time crept by as each second lasted a lifetime, but that was okay as he basked in the imagery of tumult on the TV screens.

The monitors continued to show missiles flying, as terror and panic spread like hell on wheels.

The New York scene was inconceivable. The wounds of 9/11 had barely healed when they were once again torn open. Images of people jumping to their deaths from high rise offices and apartments, bridges in gridlock from the massive outflow of cars, and complete bedlam spread across the monitors as Afshin watched in a wide-eyed fixation. One monitor in particular zeroed in on a woman standing in Times Square, holding an infant in one arm while holding the hand of the child's older sibling. Tears streamed down her face as she watched the huge display screens of Times Square confirm the warheads were on their way. The picture gave Afshin great satisfaction for he knew the world would finally be set free. He turned to Pamesh beaming. Pamesh, in turn, smiled back, bowing slightly toward his superior.

Dreaming of his new world, Afshin's smiling gaze made its way back to the monitor of the woman. As she looked at the Times Square monitors, her facial emotions turned from despair to one of utter astonishment. Afshin turned quickly to another monitor that showed an Israeli woman looking skyward. She too had taken on a look of puzzlement.

"What are they looking at?!" screamed Afshin rhetorically as his attention turned toward the monitors of the warheads. They showed the missiles in flight, but they were simultaneously turning upward, no longer in an earthly trajectory, as if a change of course had been ordered.

"What the hell is going on?" Afshin burst out, looking for a qualified answer. Other monitors confirmed that all of the missiles appeared to be off course, their direction changed in midair.

"Find the traitor who is doing this!" Afshin screamed to Pamesh, but the bodyguard in the back of the room could only offer a look of confusion, unsure how to carry out the order. Deep down, Afshin knew it couldn't be any individual since everything was under his control. He looked at the Staff as it illuminated a beautiful neon blue-green hue.

Afshin raised the live artifact up in the air with both hands. "Allah, do not forsake me! I am only carrying out *Your* will!" he screamed in pure desperation. In a panic, he attempted to meditate in order to fix the errant missiles. He sat back down on the black mat on the floor and began the Hebrew chant, but his distress prevented him from achieving the needed state of mind.

The sapphire in the Staff glowed brighter with every passing moment as Glenn and Chayim looked on in disbelief from the back of room; a glimmer of hope ignited within each of them. Their bonds of confinement had become released. Now, they were able to look at the monitors with the strength they could not muster moments earlier. The armed warheads that were once fixed to innocent targets were now turning from their programmed trajectory.

As the moments passed, it became apparent the missiles were not simply off course. They seemed to be unifying toward a very specific target. Pamesh screamed as knowledge of the new destination started to unfold.

"The missiles are headed straight for *us!*" Indeed, all warheads launched were returning to their original pre-launch coordinates; all within the borders of Iran. High above the ground the missiles lined up in succession, like pencils on a tabletop.

Afshin's day of greatest joy was quickly turning into a nightmare. A rocket gone astray hadn't occurred in decades; a dozen rockets reversing their courses back to their original coordinates was unfathomable... yet they were.

"Turn those damned things around!" screamed Afshin again. He was losing his grip. There had to be someone or something capable of diverting the warheads. He screamed out his orders again and again, but now only Glenn and Chayim were the recipients. Pamesh had run out the building in a fruitless attempt to escape his imminent doom.

The monitors began revealing images of people, once targets of Afshin's plan, crying, but this time theirs were tears of joy, relief and thankfulness. Crowds erupted into dancing in the streets all over the world. In Jerusalem, the residents of East and West, Arabs and Jews alike, gathered together in dance and cheer. They hugged one another as the sequence of events bound them for a common cause for them to come together. *This* was the new World Order. Afshin was right; he *was* the one who had brought it all about. For the first time, possibly since the Tower of Babel, the world was truly one.

Thirty seconds remained until impact. Afshin stood silent and stoic, still unbelieving that God was unhappy wanted this. Was He going to stop the warheads from striking Afshin and Iran? The missiles closed in. He reflected on his devotion to God, about how many times at rallies and demonstrations, events at which he shouted at the top of his lungs 'God is great!' had all been for naught. He reflected on The Revolution. He thought about the teachings of his elders and their eloquent speeches of hate-filled, poisoned rhetoric they belched. The message was finally comprehended- the clerics had all spoken to incite with hate and lies, not from legitimate struggle. In thirty seconds he lived his life over again... and this time, he lived it much differently.

Ten seconds left. Afshin did not know whether to repent to God or swear at Him. The anguish of his lost faith would, forever, be the last image the world would know of him.

Chayim wept now for himself and Glenn. They were relieved by what had just occurred, but they too were doomed. Sadly, they took comfort that their sacrifice would benefit many, as the warheads screamed toward them.

The Staff was dazzling in luminosity. The blue-green glow of the beautiful gem shone like a bright star illuminating the entire room. The mere sight of it caused Chayim to cry out to his lifetime friend, "My brother, my friend! I am proud and grateful to have such a great pal as you. I love you, my brother!" They fell on each other's necks and wept uncontrollably.

As they waited for impact, all the two best friends could do was hug each other, cry and give thanks to God for saving the World.

All inhabitants of the planet witnessed this last moment of the two heroes, Glenn and Chayim. They would later be written into the history books, cherished for all they were, and all they tried to do to save Humankind.

The warheads hit simultaneously across the entire country of Iran.

35

The natural response to that fateful day was as expected; the masses packed churches, mosques and synagogues in their attempts to give thanks to God. Leaders of countries filled the airwaves with talk of reconciliation and coexistence. Example after example of change emerged before a relieved world. God had shown Himself in a manner not previously seen since the giving of the Ten Commandments. Good had once again shown its superiority over evil. Love and relief and thankfulness were in abundance as the inhabitants of the world started to resume their lives. So much would be different now and the adjustment to change would be as God intended; slow and deliberate and taught over many generations.

But even with all the goodness displayed worldwide and man's love for his fellow man emerged, these were things cherished only to the majority. Evil's seed lay dormant in the dark corners of the hateful, whose obstinacies were unaltered even with the vast show of Heavenly intervention and desire. The Highest Wisdom decreed that Evil must always test mankind. Sadly, it will once again have its time to flourish.

36
Judean Desert
West of Jerusalem

The old rabbi insisted he climb to the top, along with the others. In total, there would be eight. Not seven, not nine. This was the number permitted to know the secret burial place of the Staff.

Though the rest were far younger and certainly more capable, they would not dare leave their beloved teacher to fare for himself. Three of the them walked in front, two behind and the other two flanked the old man, each keeping a slight hold on him should he slip. The entourage looked as if they were chaperoning an army general. In their own way they were, since all of them wore the traditional black pants and white shirts typical of the seminaries, not unlike soldiers. The hike was difficult. It was also sad, for it was the burial procession of an artifact that needed to become, once again, hidden from the world. It was also a recovery mission for the bodies of the seminary's former students, Yossi and Avner, along with a two-thousand year old man, whose name was not known.

Mankind still did not merit the Staff. Though the events of the past week had filled the mosques, synagogues and churches throughout the world, much work still needed to be accomplished. They taught the same message- the world needed to remember these last few days, and find a way to make lasting peace the result. The Creator had given the human race a new lease on the planet; the outcome would be up to them. Evil still lurked in the corners of Earth, the human race was now charged with eradicating it. Should they succeed, God would no longer hide Himself. In doing so, mankind would have a new relationship with the Universe's Creator, a spiritual level known only previously by Adam, the first man.

They began the ascent hours before the break of the dawn, as the cooler morning temperature made for an easier passage. The climb was slow going in the dark, as the old man's pace made what was usually a forty-five minute hike closer to an hour and a half. They stopped many times along the way, but no one minded. Each of the young students carried the proper provisions of water and food on their backs. Additionally, one of them carried, with reverence, a white prayer shawl serving as the new burial shroud for the ancient Staff of Moses. Three empty shrouds were brought along as well.

The elderly man had a difficult time at the top and required the assistance of three of his students to pull him up the final ten yards of the rock face. Once at the top, they all prayed. The two who had been here before searched for the small section of sapphire. This time, they were easily able to locate it, having witnessed its opening for the first time in two thousand years a few weeks prior.

The main stone was easily detected and the seven went right to work, using the equipment they were instructed to bring to pry it from its resting place. Once they moved the stone enough to place their hands in the crevice, progress was much easier to make an entrance large enough to fit through. Before entering, they all knelt toward Jerusalem and prayed again.

The shroud containing the Staff was passed around one last time for all to touch and to bless. Each caressed it like a priceless gem, as they were in awe of its history and humbled by its holiness. The last two in line carried it together, into the hole in the rock. Once inside, after their eyes adjusted to the dim light of the cave, they cringed and cried at the sight of the remains, new and old. Their friends Avner and Yossi, entombed just a few weeks ago, lay on the ground. The old one, whose body never decomposed, joined them. They took the Staff, kissed it one last time, wrapped it in its new linen shroud and carefully placed it once again into the crevice that had been miraculously created for it two millennia ago. Afterward, in the usual style of exiting a holy place, they stepped away from it so as not to turn their backs toward it and exited the cave.

"Okay," said one. "They're ready". They signaled for two others to enter the cave.

Two students, one carrying a shroud, crouched into the cave and retrieved the first body. They momentarily set it on the ground for the old sage. The rabbi lifted the shroud to view the face. It was Avner. The sight of his young, innocent face brought muffled cries of grief. The rabbi said a brief prayer for the dead, covered his face, and then secured the fabric around him.

The next pair entered the cave and brought out Yossi. His usual peaceful demeanor was the first striking quality of his pale body. He was a lamb in life, and also in death. He too was wrapped and blessed.

The last set of students went into the cave for the last time. Out came the young, two thousand year old sage, pale but fresh as the day he died. He was placed on the shroud, and the rabbi was again helped to the ground to bless the man and for a closer look.

"Levi, son of Jacob," said Rabbi Lindow. "You, my old friend, are truly holy, and we will now take upon ourselves the commandment of burying you as fast as possible. Bless you." The rabbi wanted to end his sentence with 'my son' since Levi was so young. But he couldn't manage, since Levi was over two thousand years old and a sage of the people. The blessing for the dead was said and Levi was wrapped up in the last shroud.

"How did you know his name?" was a question asked of the rabbi.

The cute and little old man simply said, "He visited me in a dream to thank me. Can you imagine, he wanted to thank me? What he did for the world and he wanted to thank *me!*"

All but the rabbi went over to the cave opening and took hold of the main rock to close the entrance for a period of time everyone thought about but nobody knew. They all pondered what world situation would be the next reason the cave would be opened again-destruction or redemption. Slowly they were able to move the large stone back to its age old, original location. Additional rocks were placed around it, but it still appeared as if it were manipulated. The greenish hue of the flagstone rock too was conspicuous.

Three pairs of young students each proceeded with the long and awkward procession of the bodies down the mountain. The first two remained behind to assist Rabbi Lindow down.

The morning sun was a bit brighter now, but the desert was still sleeping. Rabbi Lindow stared one last time over the Judean hills. He would never set foot here again, and he wanted to soak in that thought a few moments. The view was beautiful and solemn, the perfect scene for the removal of the two heroes of the present day and the hero of a time long past.

The old man looked over at the two and said to them, "You two must go into hiding. You will become like gods to the people. Your survival is nothing short of miraculous. We will put you some place where people will not come looking. There will be a driver waiting for you at the Ein Gedi Nature Reserve exit off

258 | Jeff Wedgle

the main road, when we start the return trip back to Jerusalem. We will drop you off there. He will take you to down to a field school in the Negev desert, about a hundred miles south of Jerusalem." He looked at Glenn and Chayim in admiration as though he was looking at the Divine.

Glenn finally spoke. "The entire country of Iran is gone. Millions of people- women and children. Why them, Rabbi, and why not us? And why not Avner and Yossi? God spared us in the nuclear attack, yet did not spare them here." Glenn had been fighting off depression since he got back. He knew the answers to those questions could never be answered; he just wanted the old sage to understand his anguish. Seventy million people had perished in a country that would be uninhabitable for many years. All of it was more than Glenn could bear, and he broke down. Rabbi Lindow put his arms around him.

"Healing takes time my son. Let God help you work that part out. After all, you've just completed His bidding. He will not abandon you." His words comforted Glenn like a warm blanket, but the sobbing continued.

Chayim stood watching the two of them hugging. He felt the despair too, but the years of devotion to his faith gave him the training to sort through it much better than Glenn.

Glenn wanted so much to talk about their experience. His face bore the beginnings of a thick black beard with traces of premature graying in the chin. The last thing he had remembered was the thunderous roar of the incoming missile striking very close by. A massive wave of intense heat hit them, but after that everything went black. The next thing they knew they were standing together in Reb Meir's home in Jerusalem. Only Reb Meir witnessed their miraculous return. But as he gazed upon the shine of the Divine his soul left his body. Thus, no witnesses were around to explain how Glenn and Chayim, who had been bound together in a warehouse in Iran, suddenly appeared. But, they were there, saved by an act of God. The Staff was with them.

The descent was unhurried as the rabbi dragged his aged and bony legs down the hill. Glenn and Chayim were in no hurry to go anywhere, knowing they were bound to go into hiding and the bodies had been recovered. What lie ahead was uncertain at best. They could never leave the field-school, much less take a relaxing walk about the town. Their faces were known worldwide, and with the exception of those who accompanied them on this journey, everyone, including their families, thought them to be dead.

Once at the basin, they stood waiting by the two large white vans that carried them into the desert. When the vehicles arrived they got in and began the rocky road back. No one spoke the entire way.

*   *   *

The white vans eventually rolled into the Ein Gedi Reserve's parking lots. At the beautiful nature preserve and oasis on the northwest tip of the Dead Sea, a small broken down automobile held together mostly by rust was waiting in a parking space far away from the main lot where no other car or pedestrian was in sight. The vans rolled up next to it and parked so the sliding door of Glenn and Chayim's vehicle opened adjacent to the second van. The rabbi looked around a bit just to make sure the area was secured, and slowly opened the sliding door on the side of the van. Glenn and Chayim got out and immediately hugged the beloved old man. With emotions surfacing, Rabbi Lindow hugged them back with all the strength he could muster. They remained in the long embrace. Finally Chayim, his eyes filled with tears broke the silence.

"Will we see you again?" he asked.

"It will be a long time, but eventually," the rabbi answered. He choked up with words, but words were hardly necessary to express his feelings.

"I know," continued Glenn. "...we will miss you too."

The rabbi pulled a white hanky from his back pocket and blew his nose. "When I return to my office, I will make arrangements to notify your parents that you are alive. But you cannot have contact with them. Let the fervor of religious fanaticism calm down. To see you would create hysteria of proportions unimaginable. In the meantime, busy yourselves with study, prayer and meditation. You will find these three elements will calm you and provide you insight and guidance. Give them time, you will see. Now, let me bless you."

The two bowed for the little man to extend his hands over their heads to receive his blessing. He placed his hands on top of their heads, one at a time, closed his eyes, and silently uttered his blessings. Afterward, he put a hand on each of their shoulders.

"Go now," he choked out in a whisper as tears welled up in his eyes.

The two heroes both choked down their emotions as well. They wasted no time as they nodded their heads in agreement and got into the back seat of the old, beat up, car. They both knew that, had they waited any longer, the pain would have been too overwhelming and the uncontrollable sobbing would commence.

A gray haired, middle aged man in the driver's seat turned his head around to meet the boys. He was handsome with a kind disposition. He smiled at them as they entered his car.

"Howdy boys," he said jovially and in perfect English that carried no accent.

"Howdy," replied Glenn. "You're American?"

"Denver, Colorado. Born and raised. Finally had the time and money to move to Israel about two years ago. You guys have any bags or anything?"

Glenn started to answer, but the man was already slowly pulling out of the parking space.

"Uh," Glenn figured he'd reply anyway, "we were told that we'll be provided for when we get to the field school."

262 | Jeff Wedgle

"Okey dokey. We'll drive from here to Arad, and then about thirty miles southwest. Should take us about an hour. "

Silence met the man's last statement. Looking at their faces through the rear view mirror, he could tell this was not a happy departure, so he didn't press conversation. "Don't feel like you have to make conversation or anything like that," he said sincerely.

Glenn half smiled to acknowledge the stranger's kindness. Chayim was looking out the window, lost in thought and didn't really hear anything that was said.

After a time, the man asked a question. "So, what are you guys going to do at the field school?"

Chayim, snapping back from his far off thoughts, replied. "Just going to learn a little, take it easy. It's been a stressful couple of weeks... a lifetime, actually."

Glenn assumed the man knew who they were and was part of the whole plan to keep them from public life.

The man nodded. "I know how *that* is. Been through times like that myself. But, somehow you get past it all, pick up the pieces, and move on." Quiet returned as the car drove down the isolated highway. "Are you just coming from the airport?"

The question made the boys turn to each other in complete wonderment. Their looks were the same. *Didn't this guy know who they were?*

Glenn answered suspiciously. "No, we've been here a week."

"I vaguely remember that something big happened last week. Do you know what it was? Damn memory of mine."

Glenn didn't offer a response. Still puzzled, he asked the man a question of his own. "What's the matter with your memory?"

"What'd you say?" he said. "The engine's too loud and I can't hear from the back seat too well." He chuckled a bit. "A little too much loud music back in the single days too. My hearing is almost as bad as my memory." The grin on his face was charming as he reflected briefly on his days of yore.

"Everyone complains about my hearing, but it's my memory nowadays. I got hit in the head with a softball bat back in Denver three summers ago... I think. Maybe four or five, who remembers? That's what they tell me anyway. I don't remember any of it. But now my memory's shot- can't remember a thing! They tell me that the settlement from the lawsuit is how I managed to afford to move to Israel. Now I just take it easy being a driver for hire. It's a good job. Keeps me occupied. More importantly, it gets me out of the house. Otherwise, I wouldn't get away from my computer. I'm writing a book."

Chayim lightened up a bit and smiled as he leaned over and whispered to Glenn. "Only Rabbi Lindow would have managed to find this guy!" Smiling, he turned to the man and asked him, "What's your name mister?"

264 | Jeff Wedgle

"Jeff Wedgle," the man said as he reached his hand back. Glenn and Chayim smiled as each shook the man's hand.

The old white jalopy continued down the empty road toward the field school.

About the Author

Jeff Wedgle is a twenty year student of Jewish religious texts. His many hours of listening to world renowned rabbis fed his creativity to write this fictional work.

Jeff lives in Denver, Colorado with his wife Heather and their two children, Rikki and Caleb. The family is community oriented and gives of their time and resources to communal programs of religious, secular and athletic natures.

About the Artist

Jared Steinberg is a professional, visual artist working and living in Denver, Colorado. He graduated with a Bachelor of Studio Arts Degree from Arizona State University and is a member of both The Art Students League of Denver and the River North Art Community (a.k.a. RiNo). Steinberg has exhibited his work in various locations in Colorado.

"My paintings are narrative compositions based off my perceptions of reality and recollections from my imagination. I distort the subject matter to fit within the dimensions of a canvas to tell my story. My art is intended to be an experience; to provide the viewer with a unique perspective that I, myself, am learning to see better every day."

Please visit www.jaredsteinberg.com for more information about the artist.